THE SINGER AND THE SILENT TYPE

HALEY TRAVIS

$\mathcal{I}$'d been warned at the beginning that this job would require many different talents, but I still laughed whenever I opened the door of the tavern with my knee while holding an armload of wildflowers from the field out back. This afternoon I managed to brace myself on the wall so that I only dropped two Black-Eyed Susans.

I dropped today's fragrant haul on one of the largest tables. Grabbing the scissors and a tray full of coffee mugs half-filled with water, I quickly started making little arrangements.

Iris, the outspoken and downright sassy owner of The Last Barrel, had said during my job interview that she wanted each employee to do everything they could to keep this more of a family-friendly tavern than an outright bar. Since it was the only place to socialize in this small town, her word was law.

Her philosophy was that if the women felt comfortable here, they would come more frequently. That meant more dates, involving dinner and conversation. And by extension, the men who were lined up across the bar drinking straight whiskey were more likely to behave themselves, since they had a mixed audience.

Although I'd only been working here for a month, last week I took it upon myself to add flowers to the tables. The glassware was too fragile to be used as vases, but hardly anyone used the coffee mugs in the evenings. A little white mug full of wildflowers added a charming touch to every table, like an old fashioned farmhouse. Iris seemed proud of me, agreeing that it did give it more of a restaurant feeling in here.

I didn't mind starting early to take on florist duties, since I got a ride with the cooks anyway. I was so incredibly grateful for this job, I would have done anything.

As I arranged Queen Anne's lace with buttercups, striped grass, and whatever the little purple flowers were called, I glanced around at the charming old-fashioned room. This establishment was the social gathering place of Sunset Ridge, and the heart of the town.

My Grandma Little had lived here ages ago, and when I mentioned that I needed a new place to live and a change of pace, my mother mailed me the keys to the old house on the edge of town. My Mother didn't teach me much about life, but I distinctly remembered Grandma mentioning when I was tiny was that if life wasn't working out, change locations. Now that I was living in an actual house, not a scruffy apartment with shifty roommates, I desperately wanted to stay forever.

After a lot of cleaning and scrubbing, it was certainly livable, even if everything was tragically outdated. My only dream in life had always been to sing in a band, but now I had a secondary goal of fixing up the old house a bit, and living there permanently.

Quickly wiping each table and placing a mug of flowers on each wooden surface, I loved the way the delicate blossoms peeked out of the chunky sturdy china. Perhaps that was a bit like me – a bit fragile, but trying to be tough enough to survive this world.

Tossing out the last of the floral bits and scrubbing my hands, I began polishing glasses and taking stock of the whiskey and beer levels.

So far, working at The Last Barrel had been the best job I'd ever had. In other bars, and even cafés, I was used to being harassed, grabbed, and treated like I could be replaced at any second.

Not so here. Iris had assured me that everyone in this place was family. None of the townspeople would dare misbehave, for fear of being banned for life. I'd actually seen Iris grab a man by the ear and march him out the front door, ordering his friend to drive him home or she would report both of them to their wives.

I liked that she ran a tight ship. I also liked that she was loud, and had no problem speaking her mind. I wanted to learn from her, and perhaps grow a bit more backbone.

Iris came out of the kitchen, wiping her hands on her apron. "Lorena, I have to say, you were absolutely right about the flowers. Good eye, missy."

"Thanks," I said, forcing myself to use my audible, working voice instead of my usual whisper.

"The special tonight is Alice's meatloaf, with carrots and broccoli. We're a little low on pie, so push the chocolate cake if you can."

"Okay," I nodded. "Is there anything different this weekend because of the rodeo?"

She rolled her eyes to the heavens, her big blonde curls shaking slightly. "That's right, darlin'. It's your first rodeo, isn't it?"

I nodded. Apparently the rodeo coming to Sunset Ridge

every year was a huge deal – almost like a county fair. It brought the entire town together.

"You saw the schedule, right?" she asked.

"Yes," I said, glancing at where it was taped over the wall phone.

The rodeo's opening ceremonies were this evening, but they were short and everyone would be coming back here for a beer afterward. Then Saturday and Sunday we didn't even open until the rodeo finished at five, and we were expecting half of the town to be here. Iris had even set up patio furniture and roped off an area outside the front window to create more seating.

"Don't look so nervous," she grinned. "It's good to have a bit of excitement around here. You're going to watch the main events on Saturday, right?"

"I think so," I said. To be honest, I felt odd going alone, even though I would probably find people there that I knew. It was strange being the new girl in a place where everybody had known each other, their parents, and their parents' parents for years.

Iris had been helping me to become accustomed to the town, pointing out the best vegetable markets, places to avoid, and people to avoid, like the local preacher's wife, Verity. Apparently, she was a savage gossip and found something negative to say about absolutely everyone. I was used to city folks being uptight, but I'd never heard of anyone being as nasty as this woman.

Luckily, since liquor was a sin, she never came to the tavern. Thank goodness. It was hard enough to make a point to be friendly with strangers without having someone breathing down my neck, trying to find something cruel to say at every turn.

We had had a bad beginning right from the start. Reverend Simon Jones, the minister of the tiny church in town, had showed up on my doorstep unannounced at eight in the morning with his wife in tow the day after I moved in. I had been wearing nothing but short shorts and a tank top, since that's what I'd slept in, and besides, I'd never lived in a place where someone would show up without calling first!

But from the look on Verity's face, you'd think I'd intentionally flashed her husband. I'd been hearing fragments of gossip and outright lies about myself ever since.

"I know it's hard being new," Iris said kindly, as if she could read my mind, which honestly seemed to happen quite often. "A little time, and you'll get the hang of meeting people around here. Everything gets easier with practice, right?" She grinned. "I'm sure the very first time you picked up the guitar you were completely dreadful."

I laughed out loud, surprising us both. "That's true," I agreed.

"Oh – I moved your guitar to the storeroom. I hope that's okay."

"Sure. Thanks so much."

I had been worried about my guitar in my grandmother's house, since it was so incredibly dry and dusty from being shut up for so long. So I left it here at the tavern, practicing when I got here before my shift. Since I got a ride most days with one of the cooks or dishwashers, and their shifts started earlier, it was perfect.

It was actually more helpful practicing here than I'd realized. My stage fright was almost comical. But years of waitressing had forced me to get over my nerves. Now that I was an outsider, meeting an entire town at once, it was another round of training myself to be outgoing and bright. The whole, 'fake it 'til you make it' philosophy.

Playing in the tavern when the only people around were back in the kitchen was good practice. I was still tingling inside from the day Iris had told me that she thought I had a lovely voice.

A few truck doors slammed in the parking lot, and I looked up to see a few of our regulars arriving at exactly the moment we opened.

Iris laughed, "I love a man on a schedule," she said. "A steady, predictable man is worth his weight in gold." I nodded, as if I knew a darn thing about men whatsoever.

Rushing to unlock the front door before they reached it, I flipped the wooden sign around to say "Open". I went back behind the bar to polish glasses while Chet and Glen headed for a table in the corner.

As soon as I had them settled with a couple of beers, I headed back to the bar, feeling a strange prickle between my shoulder blades before the front door opened again. Glancing back over my shoulder, I always felt like he was looking away just as I looked toward him.

Cody Travers. The tall, quiet man with shoulders the size of a barn. Everyone seemed to leave him alone, as if his silence was somehow a warning to keep away.

But I felt like I could see below the surface. From the way he moved, slow but almost graceful, I had a feeling he was just a guy who appreciated stillness. Someone who had nothing against other people, but just preferred his own company.

I didn't see him for the first two weeks I started working here. Then last week he came in for dinner twice. This week he came almost every night, sitting at the end of the bar in front of my station.

Even though I'd always been a bit shy around people, I found it easier to talk with Cody, since he didn't seem to want to speak very much himself. There was no reason to yatter on to him. It was simple. Even in the din of the busy tavern, it felt like we could be quiet, sharing a little smile now and then.

I'd heard that he used to be a cowboy, with a stable of horses, but now he did construction or something. Whatever he did, it made him incredibly muscular, with a deep tan that was sexy as hell.

It was strange how my stomach tightened whenever he was close. Those dark, piercing eyes, and slightly wavy black hair made him look far more intense than he actually was. He honestly didn't seem to realize that he was the most handsome man in town.

The thought of having a man in my life was a delightful yet unrealistic thought, like winning the lottery. I never seemed to be in one place for very long, and was rarely in the right place at the right time. Now that I wanted to stay here for years, I had started to think about it a bit more seriously.

I could see through the front window that more cars and trucks were pulling into the lot. With extra people from the rodeo in town, it was certainly going to be a busy night.

"Hello, Lorena," Cody's gruff voice said formally as he took his seat, slinging his denim jacket over the back of the high stool. I tried not to stare at how perfectly his black t-shirt stretched across his chest, and around his biceps.

"Hey, Cody. Dark stout?"

"Yes, thank you." As I poured his beer, a tiny smile played at the corners of his lips. I often wondered how soft they were, surrounded by his rough stubble.

Forcing myself to look straight into his eyes as I placed the glass in front of him, he stared at me for a moment before murmuring, "Thanks, Lorena."

"You're welcome. Would you like a menu?"

His gentle smile flashed straight through me, my fingers clenching my apron nervously. "Nah, if you could please put in an order for the special in about half an hour, that would be great."

"Okay, sure." He was staying here for the whole night, it seemed.

My heart began to flutter as I grabbed two menus and a water pitcher, heading to a table with two men who were obviously out of towners. As I walked by Cody, I could feel his eyes on me, making my fingers twitch. Pasting on a smile, I'd have to ignore him and focus on the customers. I needed every darned tip I could get, so that I could manage to hire someone to do a bit of work on my house before it completely crumbled around me.

Handing the menus to the two rough-looking men, I tried not to frown at the obvious way they checked me out. I was used to creeps in the city, but not here.

"Good evening, gentlemen," I began, handing them the menus with one hand, then picking up one of their glasses to pour some water. Iris said we should always be careful to start people off with water so they didn't hit the liquor harder because they were thirsty.

A loud crash as someone dropped a plate in the kitchen made me jump, sloshing the pitcher of water all over the front of my white t-shirt. Looking down in horror, I realized everyone in the room could now clearly see the outline of my lacy peach bra and rather large breasts.

The men in front of me locked their eyes on my chest. "Wow, darlin', if you wanted a bigger tip, you could just say so," one of them chuckled.

The chill of the water was making me start to shiver, but then I felt his hand on my ass. "Baby, for a lap dance, you'll get an even bigger tip."

Every pair of eyes in the room fixed on me. Verity's best friend Esther was already texting her the news. I completely froze, too horrified even to burst into tears.

*M*y body moved without thought. I watched a stranger place his filthy hand on my angel's sweet round ass, and the next thing I knew, I was holding him by the throat, shoved up against the wall.

I knew people were staring. I also knew that I shouldn't be tightening my grip quite so hard. But nobody behaved like that in my town, especially to Lorena.

"You will both leave now, and never come back," I said, my voice sounding icy, even to me. Dropping him like a sack of potatoes, he hit the floor with a grunt, looking shocked as hell.

His friend dragged him out the door and into their truck, taking off like a shot. I moved just as fast, wrapping my jacket around Lorena to cover her, and slipping her out the back door to the side where I always parked my truck.

I brought her around to the passenger side door so that she was hidden from view, and dug into my duffel bag.

"Thank you," she said softly. Everything about this sweet girl was soft. Her bright blue eyes, honey blonde hair, and endless curves that were starting to haunt my waking life as well as my dreams.

"I always keep extra clothes in my truck," I explained, pulling out a clean black t-shirt and handing it to her.

"I've noticed you always wear the same shirt."

"The only difference is the level of dirt," I chuckled, trying to put her at ease. The poor little thing was trembling, and it was physically difficult not to pull her into my arms. "Get that wet thing off before you catch a chill," I said, turning my back to her. There were no windows on this side of the tavern, so she was well hidden between the door and my body.

I heard her shuffling, then a tiny laugh. "It's sort of huge."

I turned back to see my shirt hanging on her like a tent. "Hold still." Whipping out my pocket knife, I slashed a line at the side from just below her waist to the bottom hem. Tying the two ends in a knot at her side, it gave the shirt some shape. It was pure hell not to place my hands on those lush hips.

"There you are," I smiled. "You look like a sassy little tomboy."

"Thank you," she said, looking up at me. There was something new in her eyes. After two weeks of trying to keep my distance, here she was inches away from me.

I shouldn't be speaking to her. I shouldn't be growing attached. But damn if I didn't need her, to be holding every inch of her sweetness against me. I felt my mouth fall open to speak, then snapped it shut again.

"Please," she whispered. "I know you don't talk much, but I'd like to hear everything you have to say."

I reached out to tighten the knot at her waist and tuck the extra fabric under, and didn't even realize it. "I'm sorry," I muttered.

"It's okay." Her eyes sparkled, looking so sweet and innocent that the urge to kiss her was almost too much to take.

"How old are you?" I asked.

"I just turned twenty-two."

I almost breathed a sigh of relief. I was much too old for her, and that was that.

"How old are you?" she nearly whispered. Her pretty eyes looked tense, as if she was forcing herself to ask the question.

"Thirty-eight," I said, hearing how gruff my voice sounded and trying to soften it.

Lorena nodded, smiling sweetly. "That's a good age," she said thoughtfully. "Young enough to be tough and strong, but old enough to know what you want, and how to get it."

Was she flirting with me? It had been so damn long that I actually wasn't sure. But then she gripped my arm. "Thank you for saving me," she said. Her sneakers shuffled forward a bit, as if she was trying to decide what to do.

Taking a deep breath, I tried to stay cool headed. "You should feel safe here, Lorena. Those guys were from out of town. No good man would behave like that."

Instinctively holding out my arms, she stepped in for a warm, tender hug. I had meant it to be a comforting gesture, but it instantly became much more. It was too hard not to nuzzle her sweet, soft hair, so I gave in. Lorena made the softest murmur as she snuggled tightly against me.

Then her head tipped up, bringing her lips just inches from mine. My shoulders twitched from the effort as I tried not to lean in, and failed. She paused, then her eyes closed gently as she stretched up to meet me. I kissed her softly, afraid to be anything other than gentle with this precious girl.

Her lips parted as the kiss deepened, and I swear I heard a soft moan. We fused together, my hands gripping her full hips, her perfect ass. She kissed just like she did in my dreams. Then I heard a hard-soled boot tapping on the concrete beside us.

We jumped apart, spinning around to see Iris looking at us with a delighted smirk. "For the record, I saw nothin'. I keep things to myself. But I see you've found a dry shirt, missy, so maybe you could get back to work."

Lorena's fingertips brushed my hand before she murmured, "Thank you, Cody." She followed Iris inside, leaving me to stare out at the streaks of sunset overtaking the sky, trying to figure out what the hell just took place.

She kissed me. Or I kissed her. I couldn't believe it actually happened. Looking down to see my hands slightly trembling, I almost laughed at myself. I'd worked with huge animals, rough men, extreme equipment in dangerous conditions, and nothing ever rattled me. But one kiss from the girl I'd been crushing on hard, and I felt like I'd been struck by lightning.

'd always known that the world was a strange and wondrous place. But to go from admiring my crush to kissing him out in the parking lot was a bit much to take. I felt like I'd be blushing for the rest of the night, but I knew that nobody else saw us. Iris tended to gossip about positive things, never personal things.

"Are you all right?" Iris asked, looking worried. "I heard that some guy grabbed you, but Cody took out the trash."

"I'm okay," I said, my voice sounding tiny. "It happened more than once when I worked in the city."

She turned to face me, her long beaded earrings swinging. "I'm sorry that's ever happened to you, but it should never happen here," she said sternly. "If we weren't so slammed tonight, I'd tell you to go home and shake it off."

My hands flew up in protest. "No, really, I'm fine. Thank goodness Cody had an extra shirt, so I don't have to entertain everyone with a peep show."

She handed me a fresh apron, laughing lightly. "I like your attitude, Lorena. It should be a good weekend for tips, so let's all just hustle hard." She patted me on the shoulder as I went back out to the main room.

I caught a few glances of sympathy from the women, but the men didn't look at me unless I was directly asking them about their order. Maybe they were embarrassed that they had gotten an eyeful of my lace-covered boobs. I certainly tried not to think about it, rushing around, pouring beer and smiling as if nothing had happened. Cody was back at his favorite spot, flashing me sneaky smiles now and then.

Even though the bar was extremely busy, the vibe stayed fun and friendly. Iris had everything in this place down to a science. I swear, she must have been studying bar psychology for years, or maybe it was just in her blood. Everything she did, there was a reason for it.

I knew that today's special was chosen because it was everyone's favorite. She often did this to get some food into people so they didn't just drink.

There was a small window near the front that was open, and one directly across from it at the back. This created a cross breeze to keep the air fresh. Apparently, if some people overheated, it got them feeling antsy and riled up.

There was one thing that we never wanted in a bar full of rough cowboy types – a fight. It scared the women off, and usually ended up breaking something expensive. There had been no fights since I'd been working here, but Alice, one of the cooks, told me that there had been a few doozies now and then in the past.

The sound system was playing mellow country music, mostly oldies. Iris was the only one allowed to touch the volume. If it was too quiet in the room, everyone could hear everyone's conversation, and she said that just triggered bad vibes. But if the music was too loud, people had to raise their voices to talk to their friends. This created aggression, she claimed.

I enjoyed a wide variety of music, but my voice was particularly suited to country. My biggest dream was to sing with a country band, and now that I was actually living in the country, I was going to find a way to make it happen.

There was no sense in me ever dreaming of becoming some sort of pop star with a big record contract. They tended to look like fashion dolls who lived in pink Malibu beach houses, not clay fertility dolls with big breasts and wide hips. Whatever – we can't help the way we're born.

But my voice was a gift. Every music teacher and vocal coach I'd ever studied with had told me that. All I had to do was ditch the stage fright and get out there to find a band who needed me.

Running around the bar, I often found myself singing along to various songs as I approached people's tables with their drinks and food. I found it was a great way to break the ice, and they would often sing along for a moment with me.

It finally seemed that everyone in the room had every-thing they needed for a minute, so I dashed back to the bar where Cody sat. He watched me pouring myself some ice water and dropping lime slices into it.

He smiled as I took a few sips. "Drinking on the job?" His deep voice was too sexy for his own good.

"Yes, the lime makes me tipsy, so look out." I stopped myself from clapping a hand over my mouth. Was I actually flirting with him? What on earth was wrong with me today? Or was I still high from that incredible kiss?

He seemed to like it, nodding and chuckling. "Can I get you another beer?" I asked.

"Actually, I'll take a coffee, thanks."

Pouring quickly, I brought it over, as he waved away the cream and sugar. With a tilt of his head, he urged me to come closer. "I was wondering if maybe I could give you a ride home tonight," he asked softly.

Maybe he knew that I usually got a ride home with the kitchen staff. Come to think of it, he always sat right in front of the phone and the schedule. "I'll be here pretty late," I said, "But if you don't mind waiting..."

"I don't mind at all," he said quickly. "I'd like to make sure that you get home safe, especially with so many strangers in town this weekend."

My gigantic grin seemed to amuse him. As I tried to think of something saucy to say, there was a tiny buzz, and the music stopped.

Glancing up, I saw that Iris was already pushing buttons on the sound system, giving her head a shake. She grabbed her phone from her pocket, and I assumed that she was calling her son Gary, who had set up the system for her.

I instantly whipped around the room, checking on everyone, pretending that everything was perfectly normal. After fetching a few more desserts and drinks, I saw that Iris was waving to me.

"It's a blown fuse," she said the second I was close. "Gary said the sound system was on its own circuit, and since that's the only thing that's down, it must be it." I nodded, knowing that in this ancient building, things were bound to be unstable.

Iris was giving me a very strange look. "How do you feel about grabbing your guitar and playing some old favorites for twenty minutes until he gets here?"

The air in my lungs suddenly felt stuck. "You...you said you don't have live music in here because it's too loud. Because it makes other people raise their voices, and get all aggressive..."

She stepped closer, patting my shoulder gently. "That's with a full band, with drums. Your pretty voice and quiet guitar in the corner will keep everything light and airy. You can play anything you like. All of your favorites."

"I can't…I mean, what if people don't like it?"

Iris put her hands on her hips far too high, as she did when she was laying down the law. "My customers will like what I damn well tell them to like," she laughed. "It's just for twenty minutes or so. Half an hour, tops. Will you be my little superstar?"

My chin dipped up and down, as I realized that I really had no choice. This was one of those trial by fire situations, and I could either step up to the occasion or hide like a scared child.

Looking around the room, the only empty place where I could really set up was at the end of the bar between Cody and the window.

"You're right," she said, following my gaze. "You can sit on a stool so you're raised up a bit, and the lighting is nicer by the window, since the patio lights are beaming in." She raised her perfectly arched eyebrow and leaned in to whisper. "And your fan club is right there for you."

I nodded again, taking a deep breath. "I'll go get my guitar," I said quickly, marching down to the stock room before I could change my mind.

As soon as I was safely hidden, I did a couple of quick throat opening exercises. I didn't have time to do a full vocal warm-up, but since I'd be singing quietly, hopefully I could just wing it.

As I tuned my guitar, I tried frantically to think of all the compliments I'd ever received from vocal coaches, my guitar teacher, and my family. My mom loved the way I sang men's country songs, putting a softer angle on them. I could get through this. It would be good for me, I tried to tell myself.

Walking back into the bar, I forced myself to smile. Iris already had a stool in the corner for me, and had placed my water glass at the end of the bar.

As I passed Cody, he took my hand, pulling me close to murmur, "I can't wait to hear you sing, gorgeous."

Nobody has ever said anything like that to me before. I tried to smile, but I'm sure he could see my eyes were dazed. It was also such a tiny thing, but he sort of held my hand in front of everyone. My stomach was flipping out for a whole new reason now.

This was a job, I told myself as I sat down. Happy customers, mellow customers. Maybe nobody would even realize that it wasn't the sound system, since they were all more interested in their own conversations.

My hands were shaking as I took a slow, deep breath. Looking up into Cody's deep, soulful eyes, I could see that he was rooting for me. He could easily see that I was nervous, but he was going to stay there and smile at me, making sure that I was calm.

No man had ever taken care of me before, and suddenly it seemed like his only focus was me. It was strange, but made me feel a tingle of happiness deep inside.

Strumming quietly to start, I kept my volume very low, so the music sort of snuck up on people gently. As I began to sing, I noticed people looking around the room, as if wondering where the sound was coming from. Eventually, most of the eyes landed on me. A few of them looked absolutely shocked. I guess nobody expected the shy new girl to be a performer.

As I sang a bit louder at the chorus, I snuck a look in Cody's direction. His mouth was actually hanging open in surprise.

When I finished the song, I intended to go straight into the next one, but was interrupted by a boisterous round of applause.

My cheeks felt like they were on fire. "Thank you, folks." I began another tune that I knew was a favorite with the ladies in the bar. I'd heard most of them quietly singing along here and there.

Just before the chorus, I called out, "Sing along if you know it," as if I were accustomed to this sort of thing. To my absolute delight, they did. If I hadn't been singing, I would have choked up. A room full of people were singing along with me and my guitar. It was the warmest, most beautiful feeling I'd never experienced with a huge group of people. Their smiles would have knocked me over if I weren't so focused on the task at hand.

This time the round of applause was even more enthusiastic. I glanced quickly to Iris, but she was grinning and nodding, so I assumed a little bit of rowdy behavior was acceptable. I also noticed that Esther looked perplexed, and had actually stopped texting for a moment.

A few songs later, I saw Gary rushing in to speak with Iris, then run downstairs to the fuse box. I almost didn't want to stop, especially since Cody was positively beaming at me from just four feet away. I'd never seen him smile so much. I couldn't believe that he was so fixated on me, in front of everyone.

My stomach fluttered again, but I forced myself to keep going. "This might be my last song," I said, "So sing along and think of someone you love."

I broke into a good old heartbreaker, one that I knew showcased my voice to the fullest. But this time nobody sang along. I saw that men were grabbing their sweetheart's hand across the table, and girlfriends were murmuring quietly to each other. The single men were staring at me as if I were telling them the secrets of the universe.

Cody's eyes blazed. He was staring at me with a strange intensity that I could only describe as hunger.

As I finished the song, the applause almost made my ears

ring. Iris gave me a little wave and shrug, but I wasn't sure what she meant.

"Is it fixed?" I asked.

"Yes, but you can keep going if you like."

I shook my head quickly, and she nodded, putting the sound system back on. I actually heard a few people in the back call out, "Aww," as if they were disappointed that I was finished. But my hands were starting to seriously shake, and I didn't want to push my luck.

Sliding off the stool, Cody took my arm. "Wow. I had no idea."

I felt myself blushing furiously. "Yeah, well…surprise! I'm a singer."

"You have the most beautiful voice I've ever heard," he said quietly. "Honestly, Lorena, I'm stunned." His hand flashed out to give mine a squeeze.

We just stood together for a moment in our own imaginary bubble. "I have to put the guitar away and get back to work," I said quickly.

"Of course," he smiled, as I rushed away.

 was already shaken to the core just at the thought of asking such a sweet girl out someday. Now I was actually nervous about being alone with her.

I'd never felt comfortable with women. They seemed to want so many detailed things, and I just didn't have a clue. I didn't go out dancing, or know a damn thing about pop culture nonsense. The thought that I'd never find a woman had crossed my mind quite often.

Then I met Lorena. There was something peaceful about her – an elegant stillness. She might actually be content with a quiet man, who stood back to let her shine. A man who didn't want anything fancy, just her.

Lorena's talent was as remarkable as her beauty, but her sweet demeanor was the thing that made me need her the most. My gaze followed her around the tavern as she checked in with customers, always taking a moment for a friendly comment or a joke. She complimented women on their earrings and men on their whiskey choices. She always found something nice to say to everyone. Quite frankly, she was a little sweetie pie.

As she sashayed back to the kitchen, my eyes locked onto those full, round hips. God, how I needed to take her in my arms, caress that soft skin, make her mine. It was an urge so intense that it was a bit unsettling.

The evening passed quickly, as I had another beer, then another coffee. It was always awkward for me to watch men have so many rounds of hard liquor. My dad was a whiskey man, and he was usually fuzzy-headed at night when my mom wanted his attention. He was never good enough for her, and I don't think he took care of her properly.

I always swore that if I found a good woman, I would do everything in my power to care for her in every way I could. Since by some miracle Lorena was apparently interested, I would be getting to work immediately.

As I openly stared at her flitting around the room, I caught the eye of one of my regular clients, Max, who waved me over. "Cody, I'd like you to meet my son, John."

I shook his hand, smiling at the eager, firm grip of a man in his early twenties with something to prove. "John has been learning carpentry, construction, and everything right up your alley," Max said.

"Dad said that you're absolutely the best," John said. "I would love to apprentice with you, if you ever need an extra pair of hands."

"You never know," I said agreeably, entering his number into my phone.

"I'm really looking forward to some hands-on experience with larger projects," John said. "Call me anytime, day or night."

"Will do. Thanks."

"Interesting night," Max said, looking around the room. "That new little barmaid certainly has a voice, doesn't she?"

I nodded. "That she does."

"Do you know if she's single?" John asked cautiously.

There was no proper answer to that question. It was far too early to make any assumptions.

Max saw my hesitation and shook his head. "Son, I think there's someone who has his eye on her, so best not to get in his way if you're looking for work."

John put two and two together immediately, shaking his head. "I'm sorry, Cody, I didn't know."

"I barely know myself," I confessed.

We chatted about tomorrow's big rodeo events, and wondered aloud how some of the local boys would hold up against the seasoned out-of-towners.

Eventually I excused myself and went back to my stool just in time to have Lorena join me for her break. "I see you know Max," she smiled sweetly. "He comes in quite often."

"I know everyone, more or less," I shrugged.

"What is it that you do?" she asked.

I laughed suddenly, a sound unfamiliar to both of us. "I guess you could say I'm a problem solver," I chuckled. "I used to raise horses on my little farm, but there were already a lot of great breeders and trainers around here, so I started a new business. Technically, I do all sorts of construction and repairs. But there are many strange old buildings that have been renovated over the years by people with questionable skills. I've become a bit of an expert at fixing shoddy work. I also know how to get things up to code, even when it seems impossible."

I realized that was the most I'd spoken at once to anyone in a long while.

"Wow," she nodded. Then her dazzling smile just about knocked me on my ass. "It sounds like you are literally holding this town together."

"The buildings, anyway," I smiled back.

She finished her lime water, then began cleaning up her station. Iris rang the last call bell, but most people were already trudging out. They all probably wanted to get their chores done early in the morning since they would be busy in the afternoon.

It was always amusing watching Iris walking around her establishment like the belle of the ball, yet running everything with an iron grip.

Once I'd overheard one of the regulars asking her why she didn't have any security here, and she had snorted. "If I hollered for security, would you stand up?"

"Of course."

"You and at least five other men. So I've already got security handled."

Every person in the tavern had laughed at that, and it stuck with me. That was the thing about Sunset Ridge – everyone kept an eye on each other.

When Lorena was finally done, I led her out to my truck, holding her hand to help her climb up into the passenger side, and tucking her in safely before closing the door.

It was sweet that she scooted over to unlock my side for me, but then she put on the seatbelt in the middle of the bench, so that she was sitting right beside me. As we cruised out onto the road, it felt completely natural to tuck my arm around her. "You were amazing tonight," I said.

I felt her shoulders twitch. "That was terrifying," she said.

"But you said that you're a singer?"

"Yes. I want to find a band and sing regularly. I want to record, and maybe even do some commercials."

"Well, I'm hardly an expert, but I bet you'll get some work," I said.

"I just have to get over the stage fright," she said softly.

I nodded, trying to think of something helpful to say. "I remember the first time I drove up to a big job that I wasn't one hundred percent sure of," I said slowly. "My palms were sweating, everything felt itchy and too tight, and I honestly didn't know how I was going to get through the day."

"That sounds a lot like stage fright," she nodded. "What did you do?"

Squeezing my arm around her, I looked down at her pretty angel face. "I got the job done. That's all anyone can do. You do the absolute best job you can, and you deal with nerves later."

Lorena nodded. "That's what it was like tonight. It was a job, so I did it." Her hands twisted around each other in her lap. "Maybe that's the secret. If I just look at it as a job, not something so personal, maybe that will take some of the sting out of it."

"Exactly. You would never walk out on a job. You would never do lousy work."

Her head snuggled into my shoulder. "Thanks, Cody. That really helps."

As I finally turned into her long driveway, she looked up. "How did you know where I live?"

"Just before you arrived, I heard some chatter that people had been coming and going at the old Little house. This is a small town. People tend to just hear things."

After I got out of the truck, she slipped out on my side. Holding her by the waist, I swung her down, and she instantly wrapped her arms around my neck. "Thank you for all of your help today," she said, staring up at me with those magical eyes.

My hands slipped down to her hips, pulling her against me as we both melted into the deepest kiss of my life. Her mouth opened slightly, inviting me inside. Before I knew what was happening, I had her pinned against the side of the truck, her delicious lips sending flames straight through me as I caressed her sexy hips.

Lorena made a soft noise deep in her throat, sending all

of my blood south, my arousal grinding against her shame-lessly. Tipping her head up, I brought my lips down her neck, kissing along the silky skin while she quivered in my arms.

"Cody," she breathed, "do you want to come inside?"

I froze. Hell yeah, I wanted to come inside. But I knew that if I did, I would drag her to bed immediately. That was absolutely what I wanted, what I needed. But that didn't make it right. I had to prove to both of us that I deserved her. There were far too many men in this world that didn't deserve good women, and I could never do that to Lorena.

"I do want to come in, angel," I murmured, "but I think it might be better if I at least took you on a proper date first, don't you think?"

She nodded and I released her, taking her hand to walk her toward the door. "Hey," I asked, "May I take you to the–" I looked up to see the corner of her porch awning practically falling off the house. "Jesus, how long has that been falling down?"

"Oh. Yeah," she said, looking uncomfortable. "I was given my Grandma's house, and nobody had kept it up for years. So I just don't go on that end of the porch."

"If that collapses, it'll likely take part of the roof with it," I said gently, not wanting to frighten her. "Then you're going to get water damage straight into your front room."

"Oh," she whispered. I couldn't stand how worried she looked.

Wrapping my arms around her, I kissed the top of her hair. "Don't worry, angel, I'll take care of it. This is the kind of stuff I do every day. All right?"

"Thank you," she said, looking relieved. "I've been saving up every penny for repairs, so I can–"

"You can supply coffee for me," I chuckled. "That's enough." Kissing her silky lips gently, I murmured, "I'll see you soon, Lorena."

I watched while she unlocked her door, and made sure that she locked it the second she was inside, as she waved to me through the window.

Walking back and forth along the entire porch, I did a quick assessment in the near dark of what needed to be done. Although it was probably far too soon to be thinking of her as my girl, no girl of mine was going to live in a house that was falling apart.

It took me over an hour to fall asleep since I was buzzing with adrenaline. Not only had my first public singing performance gone phenomenally, but Cody was also definitely interested in me. Both of those facts made my heart pound, and I had to admit that the thought of Cody kissing me made every single part of my body tingle.

I hoped he didn't think that I had been too forward by sitting right beside him on the ride home, but I didn't want to stop touching him. After the hug that had turned into our first kiss, I didn't think I'd ever be able to stop.

As I desperately tried to fall asleep, my mind became tangled on the one point that I couldn't make sense of. I was pretty sure that he had been about to ask me on a date when he had suddenly become distracted by the horrible condition of my porch.

I hoped that he didn't think less of me because of that. I really was trying. It was just going to take some time to get the money to fix up the house.

All night I tossed and turned, thinking of what I could do to make some more money. My head began to hammer, and I wondered if I was getting a headache. Opening my eyes slowly, I realized I was hearing actual hammering.

Grabbing my housecoat and sliding on my slippers, I tiptoed out of the bedroom to look out the front window, but it was darkened. Something was blocking off both front windows, and the door.

Approaching the door, there was a sign taped to the glass, facing my side. "Fixing porch. Use back door."

Sneaking out the back, I came around to the side of the house to see Cody with two other men, bracing the fallen porch frame with a couple of huge wooden beams.

My front room had been dark because they had covered my windows and door with a thick gray fabric that looked like a worn horse blanket. I guess it was for protection so that nothing would chip the glass.

It took all three of them to slip the brace into place, so I stayed silent until they all stepped back safely. It sounded like Cody was teaching the youngest guy, pointing out every step of the process.

Cody finally noticed me, and rushed over to give me a hug. "Hey there, gorgeous," he smiled, kissing the top of my hair just in front of the messy top knot. "Sorry to wake you, but that lift was a three-man job, and I could only get the guys for an hour this morning."

"Thank you," I said. "I didn't think it was that much of an emergency."

"They're calling for thunderstorms next week, but I also couldn't stand the thought of your house falling apart with you in it," he chuckled, his hand sliding down my spine to caress my lower back. "I'm going to keep the original structure, and paint everything exactly the way it was. You'll just have four more thick posts across the front. Is that all right?"

"Of course – whatever you think is best," I said quickly. I

was so surprised that I instantly went into work mode. "You take your coffee black, right?" I asked, as Cody nodded.

He turned to call out to the others. "John, Max, how do you take your coffee?"

I rushed back into the house, brewing the coffee quickly, and carrying out three mugs, one black, and two with cream and sugar. "I could bake muffins, or make scrambled egg sandwiches if you guys are hungry?" I asked.

"Thanks, Lorena," Max said, "But we're going to be grabbing breakfast in town in about an hour."

"All right. Thank you both so much," I smiled.

I turned to where Cody was sipping his coffee. He was staring at the rest of the house thoughtfully. "The roof definitely needs to be replaced, but I think the siding could last a few more years with a few patches and a good coat of new sealing paint," he said, speaking more to himself than to me.

"I don't have a lot of money yet for building supplies," I said quickly.

He set his coffee down on the grass, pulling me into his arms for a quick hug. "Lorena, when I first saw you at the bar, I tried to stay away from you. I know that you're a sweet young thing, full of life, and I'm a quiet old codger who is already sort of set in his ways. I don't know how else to tell you how I feel about you, so just let me fix the place up, all right?"

I leaned in to kiss him, but he turned his face away. "Not on a job site, angel," he chuckled, tweaking my nose with his finger. "Why don't you go in and relax, and I'll knock when we're done, okay?"

"Okay. Thank you."

Hurrying back inside, I fixed myself a cup of coffee, then took a quick shower. I got dressed, remembering that I had to work later that night. The tavern was going to be packed after the rodeo, so I pulled on a sleeveless blue flowered sundress. It was flattering, but fell just below my knee so it wasn't too saucy, and it covered most of my breasts, to draw less attention to them.

Styling my hair so that it fell over one shoulder in waves, I was just finishing my makeup when I heard a knock at the front door.

I came out to see that the windows were now uncovered, and opened the door. Cody grabbed my hand immediately, pulling me out onto the front lawn. The other men had already left, and as I spun around, I couldn't believe how nice the porch looked already.

"Once I get the new posts and cross beams painted, and give all of the wood a fresh coat of white so that it blends together, you won't even notice it's been repaired," he said proudly.

"That's amazing," I said, giving his hand a squeeze. "I don't know how I can ever thank you enough."

"Will you come to the rodeo with me this afternoon?" he asked. As I looked up into those dark eyes, there was something serious about his request.

"I'd love to," I said immediately.

"I just have to run home for a quick shower," he said. "You can't be seen with me all covered in sweat and wood dust."

"You can shower here, and I could make us lunch?" I said. "That is, if you have fresh clothes in your magic duffel bag."

Cody nodded, smiling widely. "If you don't mind, that would be great."

He darted to his truck to grab his bag, then we went back inside and I gave him a fresh towel, pointing him to the bathroom while I went to the kitchen. Thank goodness I had picked up groceries the other day.

I heard his chuckle before he shut the bathroom door. "I think I just time-traveled to the sixties."

"Hey now," I called back, "people pay top dollar for teal

bathroom fixtures these days!" I heard him laugh again, then the water started running.

As I made lunch, I also took a moment to pack my purse and check my makeup. I almost put on lipstick but stopped myself just in time. I didn't want anything to possibly stop Cody from kissing me as much as possible. While putting on another pot of coffee, carefully running the water at a trickle so it wouldn't mess up the shower temperature, I tried not to think about the naked, muscular, wet body on the other side of the wall.

Obviously, I failed completely.

As we pulled into the gigantic parking lot by the huge stables at the edge of town, I glanced over and was delighted to see how excited Lorena was to attend her first rodeo. I couldn't believe how attached to this lovely young woman I felt already. After watching how she cared for everyone in the tavern, I shouldn't have been surprised that she made us such a spectacular lunch, waiting on me hand and foot with coffee and her special lime-spiked water.

Racing around to the passenger side to help her out, I locked the truck then took her arm. I wasn't sure if her quick upward glance was surprise or excitement. It was the first time I'd ever taken a woman on a real date, so it was sort of a big deal for me.

Back in my early twenties when I went through a party phase for about a year, there were hangouts and sleepovers and messing around, but no actual dates. I'd never met a girl that was special enough that I wanted to be seen with her, announcing that I was in an actual relationship. Today was finally the right time.

"Are we early?" she asked.

"Just a bit," I said. "But I wanted to show you something fun first."

Leading her around to the back of a makeshift barn, we went past the riders and ranchers who were getting prepared for the day's events. At the far end of the animal area was a small pen holding two baby goats, and another with three ponies.

Lorena's happy squeal pierced the air as she gripped my hand. "Oh my God! Am I allowed to pet them?"

As we came closer, I nodded to the animal keeper. "Hey, Bill. Do you mind if my girl says hello to your animals before the kids get here?"

The older man chuckled warmly. "No problem, Cody." He turned to Lorena, who had just flashed me an absolutely shocked look. For a second I worried if it was far too soon to be calling her my girl.

"Miss, it's fine to pet the ponies, but these goats tend to nibble on fingers. You can scratch between their ears, but keep your hand away from their mouths."

"Thank you," she said, making a little clicking noise to encourage the animals to come to her.

It was absolutely adorable watching her as she petted and fawned all over them. I hardly ever pulled out my phone to take photos unless I had to match parts for a job. But there I was, taking snapshots of Lorena petting a shiny black baby goat.

When she seemed to have had her fill, I called out, "Thanks, Bill," and gave him a wave so he knew we were leaving.

I led Lorena around to the main gate and bought our tickets, heading up to the stands. "You said that the animals were there for children?" she asked.

"Yes, but how often does anyone get to see baby animals if

they don't live on a farm?" I shrugged. "I just thought you'd like it, is all."

As we sat down, she reached for my hand. "That was incredibly thoughtful," she said.

I was hit with a wave of relief. It seemed like I was learning the ropes of this relationship stuff. As long as I kept her smiling like that, I would probably be in the clear. Plus, she had seemed genuinely pleased and surprised.

One thing I heard my mother complain about was that my father never took her anywhere exciting. There wasn't a lot of excitement in this town, so I was going to make a point of taking Lorena to anything new or different, even if it was for just a few minutes.

We sat together in comfortable silence for a bit, looking around as the arena filled up. Lorena waved to several people she knew, and as I looked around, it seemed that everyone was doing the same.

I nodded to a few acquaintances and clients, giving them a half-wave, almost smirking as they looked a bit shocked that I was sitting so close to such a pretty girl. Perhaps my reputation of being a silent loner was a bit more deep-seated than I'd realized.

The events soon began, and I handed Lorena a program that I had picked up by the gate. "I don't know anything about rodeos," she whispered.

"It's all pretty simple around here," I said. "When you see the horses running around barrels, that's barrel racing. When you see a guy trying to stay on a bucking bronco, that's bronc busting."

She laughed so adorably, leaning back to tap my shoulder with her head. "You're funnier than I expected," she said sweetly.

In a blink, I was kissing her. My arm wrapped around her

shoulders, pulling her against me, as our lips melted together.

Instead of seeming surprised, it felt like she had been looking forward to this all day. The feeling of her warm, sweet mouth against mine sent shocks of fire straight through my core, and I realized without a doubt that I would be taking her home tonight.

Forcing myself to pull back, I whispered, "Time and place, I suppose."

She looked up at me, slightly flushed and breathless, nodding with a devious little sparkle in her eye. "I guess we should attempt to be proper," she whispered.

As we turned back to the spectacle before us, I couldn't help noticing a few people shooting us amused glances. Whatever. Let them stare. People should know enough to mind their own business.

The races went smoothly, and a few of our Sunset Ridge boys did better than expected. When it came time in the program for the bull riding, I heard Lorena make a little gasp. "They're not going to stab him with a sword like in the movies, are they?"

"Relax, sweetie, that's bullfighting. We don't do that here." I pointed to where the bull was shifting from foot to foot in his pen as if he knew what was about to happen. He probably did. This rodeo circuit went around the entire state.

"See the man in the green shirt? He's just going to sit on the bull's back and hold on for as long as he can. The bull is going to be ornery, but he'll barely feel the weight. Then the rider gets thrown off, and the bull gets led away."

"So the bull doesn't get hurt?"

"No. Only aggravated."

"What about the rider? That must hurt when he gets thrown off."

"Yeah," I admitted. "That's part of the sport. They train for it, but everyone knows they might break something on the way down. They signed up for it, so I guess you get what you get."

As the announcer counted down the start of the first bull ride, I looked down to where Lorena was holding my hand. Her fingers were crossed. I knew that she was kind hearted, but for her to be wishing so hard for the health of a total stranger made me realize once again how unbelievably lucky I was.

The second the giant bull was released, he tore around the ring dramatically, making the entire crowd scream with delight. Lorena's mouth was open in an O as if she were paralyzed in terror. When the rider was thrown off, he rolled away expertly, and the bull was smoothly corralled back into his pen.

"See?" I said gently, nudging her shoulder. "They're experts. Nothing to worry about."

Lorena smiled at me with relief, then seemed startled, digging in her purse. It was the first time I'd seen her pull out her phone, and it was a relief she wasn't addicted to it.

"Hello?" she answered. Her eyes suddenly grew huge, as she nodded. "Alright, I'll be right there." Turning to me, she said, "Where is the barbeque area?"

I pointed to the south end. "The red tent is food, the blue tent is the band, so you might be able to hear them setting up. It's facing away from the animals so they're less likely to be startled."

"Iris needs me for something."

"Okay," I said, standing up.

"No, that's alright," she said quickly. "She probably just needs a hand – I'll bet she's checking on the food. I don't want you to miss anything."

"Are you sure?"

"Yeah – I'll probably be back in just a few minutes," she smiled.

My gut reaction was to go with her, but I also didn't want to crowd her, or seem too overprotective. It was one of the rare times in my life when I second-guessed my gut instinct. "All right then, see you in a bit," I said. I could tell that she was thinking about kissing me goodbye, but there were even more people we knew around by now.

As she walked down the bleacher steps, my eyes instantly gravitated to her sculpted legs and the sway of the incredible curve of her ass. I tried to pay attention to the excitement in the main ring as they announced who was going to ride the next bull, but all I could think about was inviting myself in for a proper goodnight kiss when I drove Lorena home.

lthough I had really wanted Cody to come with me, I was desperate not to seem like one of those help-less girls who needed their boyfriend's attention at all times. It was enough that he was already fixing my house, and introducing me as his girl.

As I walked along the path, I smiled to myself thinking about that. He called me his girl already. That lit me up on the inside in a way I'd never felt before.

As I found Iris between the red and blue tents, I saw a band setting up. According to the program, they were going to play as soon as the events were over, when people came over to this area for food.

"Lorena, thank goodness you're here," she said, grabbing me by the elbow and leading me straight over to the stage.

"Does someone need help serving the food?" I asked, confused.

A man in a shiny western shirt with a big steel guitar came over to the edge of the stage. "Lorena, this is Bobby."

"Hello," I said, shaking his hand.

"Iris says you're a hell of a singer," he grinned. "We're in a bit of a pickle, darlin'. My wife usually sings backups for us, and solos on a couple of songs. But she just called me from the doctor – her morning sickness got worse, so she's on bed rest for a week."

"Oh my goodness – is she all right?"

"Her sister is taking care of her, so she's more annoyed than anything else," he chuckled. "How do you feel about filling in for us and saving the day?"

"Oh. Um…"

My limbs felt hollow, as if my blood had disappeared. The thumping in my chest could probably be heard over the bassist and fiddle player tuning their instruments.

"She'll do it," Iris said, looking at me carefully while she nodded. "You did great last night, Lorena. And this time there's a whole band to distract people from watching you."

I nodded. That was a good point. Plus, I had always dreamed of singing with a band. To have it dropped in my lap like this was a bit of a sign. Like Cody said, all I had to do was approach it like a job. If this were in the workplace, what would I do?

"What are the songs?" I asked, trying to breathe in and out like a normal person would.

He handed me a setlist and a pen. "Put a big dot beside anything you don't know, and we'll just skip that."

Studying the list, I saw that they were all oldies and country favorites that I really did know quite well. I only made two dots, beside songs I barely knew, while trying not to listen to Bobby and Iris conferring among themselves briefly.

"You're even wearing the perfect dress," Iris said brightly.

I could hear announcements over the PA system back at the ring, as the master of ceremonies announced the barbeque tent opening and music from Bobby Decker and the Well-Behaved Outlaws.

Swallowing hard, I saw that the rest of the band were taking their positions. "Come on up, Lorena," Bobby said, guiding me to the steps at the edge of the stage. A young man in black waved me over to a microphone already on a stand, adjusting the height for me perfectly.

Luckily it was a small stage, so I could see Bobby's setlist at his feet. Placing my purse beside the amp behind me, I got into position.

"Just have fun with it, Lorena," Bobby said. "Remember, people are here for the cheap beer as much as for us. They'll never know if we're slightly imperfect."

"Hell, Bobby's whole life is imperfect," the lanky bass player chuckled. He flashed me a grin. "Are you ready to be a Well-Behaved Outlaw?"

I forced myself to smile and nod, trying to ignore my twitching fingers as I took a few slow breaths. This was a job. My boss asked me to do a job. I was going to work hard, and make everyone happy.

Half of the crowd was already coming around to mingle in front of the tents. Sure enough, as the breeze picked up, swishing my skirt an inch above my knee, I could see Verity and Esther near the back of the crowd, shaking their heads at me. Of course they would be here, judging me.

If only Cody knew where I was. There was something about him that made me feel calm and strong. Good grief – I didn't even have his phone number to call him.

"Hey there, friends and neighbors, is everyone having a great time at the annual Sunset Ridge Rodeo?" Bobby called out. The crowd cheered, coming closer as they realized the music was about to begin. It seemed like everyone in the stands was emptying straight into the field in front of us, as the number of faces kept growing.

Please don't let me mess this up, I silently begged.

"Thank you all for dropping by. Grab yourselves a cold

beer, some hot barbeque, and maybe somebody cute. I'm Bobby Decker, and these are the Well-Behaved Outlaws. Hit it, Mikey."

As the drums started, I was relieved that the first song was a classic, and that my background vocals were simply the parts that everyone in the audience would be singing along with.

Relief rushed through me as I saw Cody coming around the corner. The second he saw me, his jaw dropped open for a split second. Then his warm, handsome smile was directed at me like my own personal spotlight. He came right to the edge of the crowd, directly in front. Pointing at me, then to his mouth, then his heart, he told me to sing directly to him. I nodded, smiling back even though my lips felt mushy and numb.

As the verse rocked along and I knew my part was coming up, I realized that right now was a defining moment in my life. This split-second would thrill me or haunt me for the rest of my days. I could sing politely and get the job done, or I could let it rip, and rock these people's butts off.

Channeling every female country rocker with high hair and sequins, I started singing, but realized it was a bit too soft. By the second chorus, I swallowed hard, and forced myself to look into Cody's eyes, singing directly to him. By the third round, I belted that tune like I never had before, even putting a little throaty vibrato on some of the longer notes.

Bobby's head spun around, his eyes wide as he nodded in absolute delight. Iris shot me a thumbs up. I saw several of my regular customers elbowing their friends and pointing to my corner. It was a strange feeling to have so many eyes on me, but it felt mostly positive, except for the two judgmental women in the back, obviously glaring and muttering.

When the song finished, the applause almost made me

choke up, but I couldn't let my throat close. The bass player took a few steps over to nod to me. "Damn, girl, you've got some pipes."

Leaning away from the mic, I whispered, "Thank you."

By the third song, I was actually dancing a little, just enjoying the music in the sunshine with a town full of people. By the fifth song, I felt like I'd chugged an energy drink, every muscle feeling twitchy and everything speeding in slow motion.

When the applause died out, Bobby said, "A wee birdie told me that our guest singer Lorena Little can belt the heck out of this next tune. If somebody hands me a beer right now, I certainly won't be able to sing, so she's just going to have to do it for me."

In a flash, one of his buddies pressed a bottle into his hand, as he turned to me and shrugged. "Sorry, darlin'. It's all you."

Squinting at the setlist, I saw it was one of the songs I had performed in the tavern last night and realized that's what Iris had whispered to him earlier.

This day had already been full of so many defining moments that I was almost numb from the adrenaline rush. Taking the mic off the stand, I shook the cable out behind me and walked to the front of the stage, giving the band a nod.

As the drums kicked in, I saw Cody mouth the words, "I'm so proud of you." Closing my eyes, I nodded, taking a breath. *This is it,* I nodded to myself.

And then I sang.

I sang as if I were in the shower alone. I sang like I had in the basement so many times, imagining that I was on a stage. I sang as if Cody and I were driving in his truck and I was simply belting along to the radio.

When the song ended, I opened my eyes to see a field full of people screaming and clapping.

For the first time in my life, I was so proud of myself I genuinely thought I might explode. It was just too huge of an emotion to keep inside my body. Swallowing hard, I choked back a tear as Bobby clapped me on the shoulder. "Well folks, I've been replaced."

"Don't you dare, Bobby," I said, flashing him a glare as I put my hand on my hip like Iris always did. "It's one thing to be the other woman for one song, but more than that feels like cheatin'."

The band and the crowd howled as I flounced back to the stand, snapping the mic into place and smoothing my hair as if being on stage was the most natural thing in the world.

To my complete shock, it really was.

On the ride to the tavern, I was delighted at how excited Lorena was. She had snuggled up right beside me again, my arm around her as I drove. I was torn between watching the road, glancing at the breathtaking sunset, and looking down at her sweet face. I loved watching her smile every time we passed a field of cows, and the way she sat bolt upright to read the signs on roadside stands selling vegetables or pies.

"You showed up just in the nick of time," she said, her head feeling so perfect tucked into my shoulder. "I swear I was about to have a panic attack, but then there you were." Her hand fell to my thigh, and I tried to stare ahead at the road instead of thinking about that.

"Something about you makes me feel stronger," she said thoughtfully. "Isn't that funny?"

"I want to be there for you, anytime you need me," I said quite seriously.

"Well, I needed you today, and there you were," she giggled. "I can't quite believe I got through it. It was weirdly satisfying singing while knowing it was being carried straight across a whole field."

"You sounded incredible. I couldn't believe how funny you were, and so relaxed," I said, flashing her a grin. "It was amazing how sassy you were with Bobby on stage."

She turned to me quickly. "Just so you know, the reason I was called to fill in was because Bobby's wife is on bed rest for morning sickness. So it's probably a one time only type of thing."

Nodding slowly, I said, "To be honest, I'm relieved to hear he's married after seeing the two of you being so comfortable together on stage."

I felt her hand on my arm. "If that's jealousy," she said in a tiny voice, "Please don't even bother. If I have you, I'll never look at another man as anything other than a coworker or friend."

Pulling into the tavern lot, I threw the truck into park as she tore off her seatbelt and jumped into my arms. Our kiss was pure fire. I already had her pulled into my lap, stroking along her outer thigh and hip, holding her body to mine.

My hand slid into the back of her silky hair, angling our kiss until it was so deep, so all-consuming that the windows might fog up, even in this heat. Finally tearing myself from her lips, I kissed down her soft throat, nuzzling her collarbone until she moaned.

"Cody, nobody has ever made me feel like you do."

"That's because you're mine, angel. Can you feel it?"

She ground into the stiff bulge in my pants with a little giggle. "I can feel it."

"Damn, you're saucy," I growled, yanking her lips to mine.

Her soft gasp, her soft tongue, her sexy, curvy body in my hands...there were only a few cars in the front lot. I wondered if we should risk getting busy right here.

Lorena shifted her hips, brushing her panties across my

jeans, her eyes so wide and innocent. A shudder ran through me as I realized how innocent she likely was.

Bringing my mouth to her ear, I breathed, "Lorena, you have no idea how much I need to thrust my cock up into your heavenly little pussy right now. So we need to stop right this second before I make you very late for work." I honestly had never said anything like that to a woman before.

Instead of pulling away or slapping my cheek, she kissed me more deeply, her ass rocking as she ground harder. Goddammit, she was as turned on as I was. It took every single ounce of my mental strength to pick her up and set her beside me. "You know I want you. But not here."

"I know," she giggled, then looked a little embarrassed. "Sorry."

Staring at the windshield, I tried to will my dick to settle down, then we jumped out and went into the tavern.

I could hear a bunch of frantic voices in the kitchen, as they were likely preparing for a very busy night. "Is there anything I can do to help?" I asked.

"I don't think so. I'll let you know what the special is as soon as I do."

As Lorena started wiping down the bar, I looked around the room. "Aren't there usually flowers on the tables?" I asked. "Or maybe that was a temporary thing. I think it just started a few weeks ago."

Lorena rolled her eyes and shook her head at the same time. "Darn it. I forgot. The flowers were my idea – to keep it cozy in here. But I don't know if I have enough time today."

"Were the flowers delivered?"

"No – I just got in from the field out back."

"You fix up a tray of mugs and water, and I'll play florist for the night," I said.

"Really?" She looked more surprised than usual. Those innocent eyes instantly made my pulse surge.

"Don't worry – I can manage."

Twenty minutes later, the bar was filling up as I was placing a mug full of buttercups, white frilly lace things, and striped spikey grass on every table. Lorena had declared me her 'backup florist', and anything that made her smile like that was just fine with me.

I didn't mind that a couple of acquaintances chuckled when they noticed when I was up to. Over the years I'd seen many guys doing many strange things for their women. This was certainly no different. Except this time it was me, and I actually had a woman of my own.

Even though it was very early, I already felt like Lorena was the one. Everything about her made my heart speed up. I was looking forward to long conversations with her just as much as I was looking forward to getting her naked.

It was fascinating to me that the people I had mostly ignored over the years were now chatting with me as if it were the most natural thing in the world. Maybe I'd put up more of a wall than I realized, and now that people had seen me with Lorena, it had somehow brought the wall down.

Did having a girlfriend make a man seem more approachable? Or was it that I felt more chatty and relaxed because she was now in my life?

The tavern was packed, and Lorena brought two plates of tonight's special to my end of the bar. Placing her plate on the lower inside counter, she bent down to sneak a few bites here and there. "We're not supposed to eat in the main room while we're working," she explained, "But since I was so busy right before my shift, I think Iris will forgive me."

"Absolutely," I said, winking to Iris where she was obviously noticing from the other end of the bar, and just giving a shrug.

I was so glad that Lorena worked in a place where the staff would look after her. But I really didn't like her having to rely on the folks from the kitchen for a ride home every night. As I ate my chicken and corn stew with sourdough biscuits, I looked around at the townsfolk. She was pretty safe here, but I didn't like her living alone without her own car.

After I finished my meal, I realized this was something I could take care of for her. Crossing the room, I went over to a couple who were having a drink in the corner. "Hello George, hello Esther. Do you mind if I interrupt for just a moment?"

"Not at all," George said warmly. "I'd offer you a chair, but the Barrel is packed tonight." I nodded, forcing myself to smile at his pinch-faced wife.

"I wondered if you have any small, reliable cars in right now. Doesn't have to be fancy."

He instantly flashed the grin that was the hallmark of the ads for George James' Used Cars, a tiny dealership that was actually on the front field of his small ranch. "Actually, I have three in right now that would fit the bill." Then his silver hair cocked to the side. "You've got that big truck that's only two years old, am I right? What do you need a new car for?"

"I'm asking for a friend," I said cautiously.

"Well, thanks for thinking of me. Y'all give me a holler soon and come test drive anything you like."

"Thanks, George, I appreciate it," I said, shaking his hand.

Someone behind him called his name, and he jumped up to say hello. Esther had been giving me a pointed side-eyed glance during our entire conversation, and as I started to leave, she stood up to speak quietly in my ear.

"I hope you're not going to waste your time on that little tramp Lorena," she hissed under her breath. "She's been here just over a month and has already been seen getting fresh with several men."

I somehow managed not to laugh in her face out of respect for George. "Really? What men?"

"You saw her in here last night, giving a peep show to those out-of-towners," she glared.

"If you think she spilled water on herself on purpose, that's just sad," I said. Suddenly I realized that her meanness was probably not just her own, but coming from the preacher's wife and town busybody Verity as well. That woman had always truly hated anything new in this area. New was automatically evil in her mind.

"Any decent person would feel sorry for her for accidentally making a spectacle of herself," I said, trying to keep the anger from my voice. "You and Verity can just mind your own business, or I'll be telling your husbands about the nasty gossip you spread."

I glanced to see that George was still talking to a man off to the side, and had no idea that his wife was blushing furiously.

"You wouldn't dare," she spat. "We are just trying to keep the men of this town wholesome and keep hussies away from them."

"I'm serious, Esther. This foolishness stops now, or I'll take it straight to the preacher so that he can pray for your lying, gossipy souls."

She sat down as quickly as if I'd slapped her. To be honest, the thought had almost crossed my mind.

As I went back to my stool at the end of the bar, the positively horrified expression on Lorena's face nearly broke my heart. "What was that about?" she asked.

"Nothing important." She didn't seem convinced, but she was too busy to ask further.

I was content to sip my beer in the corner, but kept turning to see the hugs and roars of laughter as old friends greeted each other.

Iris came over to lean beside me at the end of the bar. "Problems with Esther?"

"Not really."

Iris cocked her head, staring at me. "You keep a lot of things under your hat, don't you, Cody?"

"Yes, ma'am, I do."

"Although you're one of the few cowboys I never see wearing a hat..." she smiled at me. Then she grew serious. "You know, I consider my employees to be my family. Normally, a young girl, new in town without any real friends yet...I'd be extra protective, and feel the urge to lay down the law if I saw an older fellow getting cozy with her."

Nodding, I thought it best to just let her continue. "But I don't have to worry about that with you, do I, Cody?"

"No, ma'am. I think the world of Lorena, and intend to do everything I can to make her happy and keep her safe."

Iris patted my arm. "That's what I thought. Don't worry, I'll mind my own," she said, walking away.

Looking around the room, I saw Lorena blushing as she set mugs of beer down in front of a table of men. It took me a second to focus on their conversation through the din, but they weren't harassing her, just raving about her performance this afternoon.

Quickly turning back to my beer, I didn't want Lorena to think that I was spying on her. I couldn't help the protective urges that were overtaking me already. But I knew that men sometimes got riled up on nights like this, so I continued checking on her all night long.

The next few hours went by quickly, as I had a coffee, then one of Lorena's strangely refreshing lime waters. Iris rang the last call bell, and everyone eventually hauled themselves away into cars and cabs. The second she was finished, Lorena came over to me. "Thanks for waiting," she said. "I really appreciate it."

Slipping an arm around her, we went outside and I helped her into the truck. As soon as we started driving, she snuggled into my side in a way that made me never want to let her go.

I found myself wanting to drive too quickly, and tried to take it easy on the gas. "I was so proud of you up on that stage today," I said. "You shone brighter than the sun. It was amazing to see you let go like that."

"Thank you," she said shyly.

"I heard some of the folks in the tavern tonight telling you the same thing. I hope this means you'll be singing a lot more."

"Were you keeping an eye on me?" she laughed.

"Not really. I may have glanced a few times when you were talking to the out-of-towners, that's all." Catching her eye before I turned down the side road, I said, "I don't want to overstep my bounds, like I probably did with fixing your porch."

She laughed lightly. "It sounds like it was more of an emergency than I realized. Thanks so much for that."

I paused, driving past the fields, wondering whether it was too soon to say what I was thinking. "Of course, I don't quite know where the boundaries are yet, but I think I'd like to make things official with you," I said, pulling into her long driveway. "I'd like to be your boyfriend."

Her rosebud lips fell open. "Really?" Lorena smiled, but looked a bit tense as I parked the truck and turned to her.

"What's the matter? Please, be honest. Don't you want to be my girlfriend?"

"I do! Really I do. I'm just sort of surprised, I guess. I mean, I saw you talking with Esther."

I made a disgusted grunt that caused her to laugh. "That nosy bi... woman is pretty much the only nasty person in this town besides her crony Verity."

"So you don't listen to them?" she asked hopefully.

"Not in the slightest. I listen to you." I chuckled. "And Iris, to some extent."

Lorena smiled. "Iris is sort of the town's Mom, isn't she?"

"Yeah."

"She likes you," Lorena said, squeezing my hand. "So as far as I'm concerned, you have her seal of approval. I'd love to be your girlfriend."

I grinned, then ran around to lift her out of the truck. Holding her hand, I walked her to her front door. "Would you like to come in?" she asked softly. "I'm so wired from that adrenaline rush today that I might actually have half a glass of wine to settle down. I think I have a bottle of whiskey, if you'd like."

"I don't touch hard liquor," I said, following her in the front door and pulling off my boots. "But Lorena, I'm going to need you to ask me to leave after one drink."

She spun, her hair swirling out behind her as she nestled in my arms. "Why? I mean, would it be so terrible if you stayed the night?"

Dammit, I wish she hadn't said that first. My fingers clenched around the firm swell of her ass, pulling her tight against me as I kissed her. Her soft moan tightened every muscle in my body as I picked her up, carrying her to the couch and setting her on my lap.

"Lorena, if I stay the night," I murmured, kissing under her ear, "I won't be able to keep my hands off you."

"That's okay," she whispered, but she sounded a bit nervous.

"Angel, I can't touch you if you're jumpy about it." Yet my hand was caressing her knee under her dress, as I tried not to wander up her inner thigh more than a few inches.

She swallowed hard, looking at me with those big, bright

eyes. "Cody, I've had feelings for you from the first time I saw you."

"Really?"

"Yes. You'd just sat down at the bar, then suddenly jumped up to get the door for an older lady with a walker. You settled her at the best table at the window, pulling out her chair and listening to her ramble on about her cat for a few minutes."

"Mrs. Hartley," I said, shaking my head. I couldn't believe she remembered that.

"You're quiet, but you're so kind," she said gently. "Everyone knows that you're a good man."

Staring into those heavenly eyes, I forced myself to speak. "Lorena, what if I'm not good enough for you? What if I'm not everything you need?"

She laughed, slipping her arms around my neck and holding me tightly. "Cody, you're everything I've ever dreamed of and more. I like the way you seem to want to take care of me, but you don't want to change me."

I nodded, then she held my face between her delicate hands. "But you'll have to tell me now – are you going to be upset when I find a band to sing with? It'll probably be mostly guys, and I might be traveling a bit. You're not going to freak out or be jealous, are you?"

I shook my head. "I trust you completely, Lorena. I might ask to meet the band. I might ask for you to text me so that I know you're safe. But I'll try not to go overboard. Is that fair?"

"Absolutely," she said. "Oh!" She jumped up and grabbed her purse. "Just before the band started, I wanted to text you so you knew where I was, but I didn't even have your number." I took her phone from her, entering my name as a contact, and my number, then texted myself so that I'd have her number.

"Thanks," she said. "I was so glad that you appeared just in time. You really do make me feel safe."

Setting her phone and purse on her coffee table, I held her close to me. "You shouldn't feel safe around me when we're alone, and this near to your bedroom."

Her eyes grew wide, as her lips curled into the sauciest smile I'd ever seen. She kissed me gently, but I could feel her intention quite clearly. My hand slid up from her waist, caressing the underside of her breast. From the way she gasped softly, pressing herself into my hand, it was obvious what she wanted.

Picking her up, I carried her to the bedroom, placing her in the center of the bed. Clicking on the small bedside lamp, it gave a faint amber glow, showing off the bit of rosiness across her cheeks and the bridge of her nose from our day outside.

"You are impossibly beautiful," I said, tearing off my shirt and sitting beside her.

Her eyes were huge as she took me in. She seemed to relax as my fingertips danced down her throat, then tensed up again as I slowly reached into the front of her dress. Sitting up, Lorena unzipped her dress at the back, and I helped her pull it off completely.

I instantly unfastened her bra, slipping it off to admire her creamy round breasts. The rosy nipples were the perfect size, puckered slightly, tightening even more as I wrapped my lips around one.

"Oh," she sighed, lying back across the bed.

Sucking gently, I tried to analyze every little murmur and noise that she made. But she seemed to like everything – feather-light kisses around her cleavage, licking each nipple back and forth, even when I nibbled a bit harder, making her gasp as my teeth skimmed her flesh. I moved up to kiss her again, and an instant flare of heat shot through both of us.

"You taste so sweet, baby," I murmured, my tongue caressing the seam of her lips until she moaned, opening her mouth for mine.

Lorena's arms were around my shoulders, both caressing my skin and pulling me closer. "You feel so good," she breathed, as I cupped the underside of her breasts gently, leaning in to lick and suck them again.

Her gentle moans were driving me insane, and I shifted my hips trying to make sure that my erection wasn't pressing right against her. But as I shifted away, she leaned in, intentionally rubbing her hip against me. She was arching herself into the palm of my hands, wriggling slightly, and definitely signaling that she wanted more.

Moving slightly to the side, I slid one hand over her soft stomach, slipping my fingers under the waistband of her pink cotton panties. "Spread your legs a little for me, angel," I murmured. "Let me feel you."

She nodded, her blonde hair fanned across the pillow, and her sexy smile making my pulse throb in my cock. As my fingers slid lower, skimming along her delicate flesh, exploring every fold, I honestly wondered if a man could come without even having been touched.

Her sweet little pussy was so warm and wet, her juices slipping along my fingertips as I stroked her gently. From the way her breath caught in her throat, her shoulders twitching, I had a sneaking suspicion I already knew the answer as I asked, "Am I the first man to ever touch you here?"

She nodded, then made a soft murmur as my finger traced through her slit, spreading her inner lips.

"Am I the first man who's going to make you come in his arms?"

Lorena's eyes lit up with absolute delight as she nodded again. Brushing lightly over her little nub of nerves, her eyes half-closed as she shuddered. With each tiny twitch, I learned what she reacted to. Kissing her gently, the feeling of her gasps into my mouth made my body ache for hers.

When I figured that I had teased her enough, I slipped my middle finger inside her just a bit, softly caressing her tender clit with my thumb.

Her long, low inhale sounded like it was rattling. Her hips began to tense, and I could feel that she was nearing the edge. Then she pressed her lips together, making the strangest soft whining sound as her thighs clenched.

"Don't be quiet, baby," I murmured, kissing along her cheekbone to her ear. "Let it out. Just relax and let go for me, angel."

"Cody," she murmured, looking up at me with those huge blue eyes. "This feels so good."

"That's what I'm here for," I smiled, kissing her lightly on the lips while giving her enough space to moan into my mouth. "Come for me, beautiful."

Moving my fingers just a little faster, pressing a tiny bit harder, her stomach seemed to flutter, then she squealed against my lips.

"Damn, you are sexy, Lorena," I growled, kissing her hard and rough as she exploded in my arms, holding onto me as she shook. When she stopped twitching, I kissed her gently, then pulled away to smile at her. "That was the sexiest thing I've ever heard."

Pulling my hand away, I dragged my middle finger down my tongue while she watched me suck her juices. "May I take your panties off so that I can lick you?" I asked.

She shook her head.

Stroking her hair, I murmured, "That's all right, angel. That's enough for one night."

Lorena grinned as she sat up. "That's not what I meant. I mean that it's your turn."

I chuckled, raising an eyebrow. "What do you mean?"

"Take off your pants for me, please."

No man could possibly resist such a polite request. Standing up, I dropped my jeans and shorts, watching her eyes widen as my erection came into view.

"Oh," she said softly. "Wow."

I knew that I was a bit on the large side, but realized that she was likely more surprised because it was the first one she'd seen in person. Lying on my back, I wondered what she had in mind. Her delicate hands wrapped around the base, as she slowly, cautiously, stroked the entire length.

"I haven't been with a woman in a really long time," I said sheepishly, "So I might be a little sensitive."

"That's probably good," she said, flashing me a wink, "Since I have absolutely no idea what I'm doing."

Lorena proved herself a complete liar when she moved down between my legs, popping the head of my shaft between her perfect lips and sucking my length into her mouth. She moved slowly at first, taking her time and getting a feel for it before increasing her speed up and down.

"Sweet Jesus," I muttered, involuntarily grabbing the back of her hair, intending to slow her down. But she worked her hands and mouth together, creating pressure across the entire length of my shaft.

Feeling her tongue fluttering against my flesh was more than I could take, but she looked up at me so hopefully, obviously wanting to please me. "Slow down, it feels too good," I groaned.

She gave her head a tiny shake, then began actually sucking hard, moving quicker. Watching her smiling eyes as she seemed so dedicated to satisfying me made my entire body shudder.

"Mmm, I can't stop, angel."

Lorena's tiny nod was all it took. Her lips pressed harder, and she seemed ready to take it all. I tried to be as gentle as I could, but my fist in her hair was moving her sweet lips just a bit faster.

"Baby..." I growled, staring into those beautiful sweet eyes as everything tightened. Exploding down her throat, she blinked in surprise, swallowing quickly as I released every bit of tension in my body.

The second I could catch my breath and see straight, I pulled her up gently by the shoulders to kiss her. "I'm sorry, angel, I didn't mean to pull your hair like that. I didn't mean to lose control."

"I'm fine," she giggled. "Actually, um, I liked it. I've always wanted to try that."

I laughed out loud in relief. "Really?"

"Yeah," she blushed. "It just felt...naughty."

A girl who was so unbelievably sweet, but wanted to be naughty in the bedroom? I honestly could not believe my luck.

~ LORENA ~

I was surprised at how comfortable I was with Cody. Everything we did together just felt right, and somehow my nervousness was falling away. Then I was shocked as he flipped me onto my back, kissing down my body until his huge hands pressed my thighs apart to make room for his mouth.

My strange gasping moan didn't even sound human as it filled the room. He kissed along every bit of my skin as if he were exploring me. Memorizing my body.

His deep eyes looked up at me as his tongue began to lick steadily right where I was wettest. He stroked all the way along that magical cluster of nerves, sending sparks of pleasure straight down to my toes.

I loved that he took his time with me, not wanting to rush a single moment. I loved that he was so close to me already, so intimate and connected. As my breath began to rattle in my chest, his eyes smiling up at me, I realized that I was already falling completely in love with him.

My fingers tangled in the top of his hair as my hips began to squirm, that deep hum of desire overtaking me.

He dug his tongue in harder, lapping at me as if I were the most delicious thing he'd ever tasted. Every single thing he did made me feel precious. I couldn't help but feel greedy for wanting more, then he added the tip of a second finger, pressing steadily inside me. I pulled his tongue against me tighter until the deep, tingling heat flooded me in deep waves, my moans becoming a shriek as I came.

When I finally stopped shaking and gasping, Cody looked up and licked his lips. "I knew you'd be delicious," he grinned.

He laid beside me, wrapping me in his arms. "Wow," I whispered, shaking my head and laughing at myself.

"Do you want me to sleep here?" he asked.

"Yes. Please."

Our bodies tangled together, my head tucked into the crook of his shoulder. "You feel perfect against me, angel," he murmured, kissing the top of my hair.

"I think I'm becoming addicted to being in your arms," I whispered.

I was already drifting off, then felt his fingertips brush my hair back, tucking it behind my ear as he kissed my temple. "I'm already falling for you so hard, Lorena. Now that I know you're my girl, I'm never letting you go."

Smiling slightly, I nodded, murmuring "Mmm hmm," but couldn't even form words anymore.

Several times in the night I woke up with Cody's strong arms around me, feeling like the luckiest, safest, most treasured woman in the world.

When I woke up and saw daylight streaming in, I glanced at the clock to confirm that it was actually morning, then reached for Cody. He wasn't there.

Looking around my bedroom, I saw that his clothes were gone. Throwing on a giant old t-shirt that I used as a nightgown sometimes, I went out to the kitchen, looking around. Cody wasn't there either.

He had mentioned that he often worked very early mornings, so I searched the house looking for a note. There was nothing on the kitchen table, the refrigerator, or the front door. I couldn't think of any other logical place someone would leave a message. There was a notepad and pen right beside the front door that really couldn't be missed.

I went back to my room to grab my phone to see if he had sent me a text, and then saw his phone on the far bedside table. What on earth makes a man leave so fast that he forgets his phone?

Slumping into the kitchen to make myself a cup of coffee, I noticed that the machine was already brewing. He must have filled it and set the timer for me. I opened the cabinet to grab a mug, and the door swung smoothly. The loose hinge had been tightened.

Sitting down with my coffee, I tried to make sense of this weird behavior. Cody was such a straight-up guy. A bit old-fashioned. Almost formal. I couldn't imagine him leaving without saying goodbye, unless something terrible had happened.

Could I have talked in my sleep? Or was spending the night too much, too fast?

Whenever he was with me, he seemed like he was all in – that our relationship meant a lot to him. He must have known that I would be upset at his disappearance. Was that his point? I shook my head.

The coffee was ready, so I poured a cup, sitting down with my phone to check the weather. I also checked the Sunset Ridge community group for general news, and to see what people were saying about the rodeo.

It seemed that people were mainly talking about the rodeo events, broken records and personal bests. But there were also many people chatting about how much they enjoyed Bobby Decker's band, and the newest "Well-Behaved Outlaw".

Many people were expressing sympathy to Bobby's wife for missing the show, but lots of people were commenting on how much they enjoyed my singing. Some people, mostly regulars I recognized from the tavern, couldn't believe that a girl who seemed so quiet could, as little old Mr. Jenson said, "belt it to the high heavens."

I could have cried from happiness, but then the tears became real as I realized the first person I wanted to share that with was Cody.

I spent a few hours scrubbing the house, and working on a few little fix-it projects. After a few hours, I realized I should check my phone just to see if maybe he'd somehow called me from someone else's phone. The only message I had was from Alice, saying that she had to work early, so she'd be picking me up at three.

That was a great relief, since puttering around the house wasn't making me mellow today, it was driving me nuts. As I got ready for work, I decided I would take Cody's phone to the tavern, since he would likely look for me there.

The screen lit up as I lifted it, showing fragments of the last several texts he'd received flashing in a quick blur across the screen, from someone with the last name either "James" or "Jones".

...promise me you won't go too far...

...been around a bit, so you know how they take it...

...heavier ones always ride better – used to the rough...

What the heck was that about? I couldn't see who sent the messages without unlocking his phone, and I couldn't even call the bits of the messages back.

My blood ran cold. There was no way for me to know if those messages were sent by Verity Jones, or Esther Jones, telling Cody that I was the town slut. They likely thought it was their duty to warn him, and didn't want him to end up with an out-of-towner. No matter how long I lived here, that was how they were going to see me.

I didn't think Cody was the type of guy to listen to horrible gossip like that, but this made it abundantly clear that I really didn't know him very well yet. Falling across my bed in tears, I could still smell him on the pillow, making me cry harder.

It served me right for getting my hopes up so high, so fast. He was a wonderful man, and probably allowed himself a little fling now and then. There was no way that he could be so passionate about me so fast. It was likely part of his method of picking up women. Since he seemed so quiet, he could easily get away with it.

I wasn't sure if I actually believed that line of thought, but I couldn't think of any other reason why he wouldn't leave a note or message. He must be dumping me already.

Forcing myself to get up and fix my makeup, I changed my outfit, wanting to wear something that made me look slimmer after that message about my being heavy. A nice dark blue dress toned down my breasts, and skimmed nicely over my round hips, making my curves look more womanly, almost elegant.

Slipping a light blue rhinestone flower clip into my hair, I held my head high as I threw Cody's phone into my purse. I figured he would show up at The Last Barrel tonight. Or at least, he would know to look for me there.

If I could handle stage fright, I could handle this, I told myself as I heard Alice coming up the long driveway. Locking the front door, I pasted a smile on. There was no way I was going to let anyone see that Cody had upset me.

Singing along with the radio on the way into town, Alice

kept me entertained with her strange attempts at harmonies that had us both in stitches.

When we got to work, I found that scrubbing the tavern floor didn't drain my frustration, but it impressed Iris, so at least that was something. She came charging in almost late, looking pleasantly surprised.

"You've been scrubbing so hard I don't know which I should be more worried about, missy, the floorboards or your nails." My fake laugh only made her stare more deeply into my eyes. "What made you so upset?"

Shaking my head, I found there was nothing I could say.

"Alright, then," she said gently, patting my shoulder. "But I'm always here if you need a shoulder to cry on in the storage room, okay, hon?"

"Thank you," I said, my throat tight. "Um, how was the cook-off?"

Iris beamed. "One of the younger gals won this year – Jolene King. Just amazing. If she comes in tonight, be sure to give her a free dessert, okay? And also one for the guy who might be her new sweetheart, Rhett."

"Sure."

Iris gave me a little hug on the way by. "Hang in there, darlin'."

It was a great relief that I felt close to my coworkers so quickly. With no family other than my very distant Mother, I had been used to being totally alone in the world for a long time. It was nice to finally feel like I had a home, with people I could count on.

Getting back to work, I scrubbed each table, prepared the wildflowers, and got the room looking nice just in time to see several cars pull in a few minutes before we were supposed to open.

Iris unlocked the door and flipped the sign. "What's ten

minutes between friends?" she shrugged. "Besides, if people were in the sun all afternoon at the rodeo, they'll be parched."

Filling the pitcher, I started off the first round of customers with water. It was nice to see everyone so excited about the events this weekend. I'd been feeling sort of guilty living in this town and not knowing very much about life on a real ranch. But I learned so much about ranches, farms, horses, and cattle just by zipping in and out of people's conversations. It was fascinating. And I admired how hard working these good people were, no matter what was thrown at them.

An hour and a half later, the tavern was nearly full, and I had just served dinner to nearly everyone. Alice was going to run out of spicy cheeseburgers well before the night was through.

Rushing around was making me feel centered again, and shaking the misery out of my body. I didn't have time to be upset, or pine for some jackass who listened to terrible gossip. I shouldn't be wasting my energy on a man who said he wanted to take care of me, then took off.

As I sipped my lime water, staring at the empty stool where Cody usually sat, I realized I was becoming more angry than upset. Even though I desperately needed to go out back and have a good cry, I also needed to punch something. I'd never had emotions this huge before, and it was a strange new feeling.

Yet everything turned to love with a side order of lust again as Cody walked in the door. His face lit up when he saw me, as if nothing in the world was wrong.

I needed to jump into his arms. But I also needed to slap him so badly that my hand trembled as I set the water down.

His dazzling smile dissolved as he came closer. "What's wrong, angel?"

My mouth opened to speak, then I was suddenly gripped with terror that I was going to yell at him, even though I'd never yelled at anyone in my life. Dashing across the room at a record-breaking speed walk, I made it to the ladies' room before the tears took over.

My stomach felt as if I'd been punched. People were already going back to their dinners as if nothing was wrong, thank goodness. I was sure that Lorena wouldn't want anyone staring at her. But it killed me that she was so upset, and obviously because of me.

I decided that the best plan of action was to give her a minute, I sat down, desperately trying to think of what I did wrong. Last night had been the most incredible night of my life. At the time, it certainly seemed like she felt the same way. What could have changed between then and now?

I left for work in the morning, I ran an important urgent errand, and then I came here to see her. That was it.

Iris came over, her hands in fists, parked a little higher than her actual hips. "Cody," she said in a lower, serious tone, "Did you upset my girl?"

"I guess I did, but I have no idea how," I said quickly. "Iris, I swear I'd never hurt her on purpose. I must have just… made a mistake somehow. I'll make it right as soon as she tells me what it is."

"Get after her, then," she glared.

Nodding, I slowly walked to the ladies' room, trying to think of what the hell to say. Tapping at the door, I could hear muffled sobs and angry muttering. "Lorena, I'm coming in."

"Leave me alone," she choked.

I couldn't stand listening to her cry. Opening the door just an inch, I said, "I swear, baby, I will do as you say every day for the rest of our lives, but right now, I need you to listen."

I felt like a total heel, especially going into a place that was clearly off-limits to me. But I would have done absolutely anything to stop her tears. I entered the small room slowly to find her sitting on the counter beside the sink. I approached her cautiously, as if she were a wild animal. Since I'd never seen her upset or angry before, I honestly had no idea how she would react.

"Whatever I did, please tell me so that I can fix it," I said gently.

"How in the actual hell can you not know what you did?" she sniffled, pinning me with a glare that could have stripped paint from metal.

"Lorena, I've never had a girlfriend before. I'm sorry, but you might have to train me like a dog for a bit. I swear I'll learn to obey."

The corner of her lips twitched as if she was stifling a giggle. That was a start. Then her bottom lip quivered. "It's not my fault those women hate me, but I certainly didn't think you'd listen to their lies."

"What women?"

She handed me my phone from her apron pocket, which I had somehow completely forgotten about. "I wasn't snooping," she said quickly. "I would never do that. I was just picking it up to bring it here, figuring you needed it. But I saw some bits of texts telling you to stay away from me because I was a slut."

Opening my phone quickly, all I saw were a couple of texts from George, telling me about the cars he wanted to show me.

"And then…" she choked, "the one about how I'd ride better because I was heavier. That's just disgusting."

Finally I put two and two together, staring at the snippets of the messages she could have taken a different way. Closing my eyes for a moment, I forced myself not to laugh. "Baby, those texts had nothing to do with you."

"Then why did you leave me this morning?" she demanded.

"I didn't leave you. I just went to work. I made myself a coffee first, then put it on the timer for you, so that yours would be fresh."

"You didn't leave a note," she whispered.

Dammit.

My hand ran through my hair and I realized the heel of my boot was tapping nervously against the floor. "Shit, baby, I'm so sorry. I didn't think. There was something I needed to take care of, and I just jumped up and got cracking. It's the way I've always been."

She bit her bottom lip to keep it from quivering, but her sweet eyes looked hopeful. "You really didn't take off on me?"

I reached out to take her hand, and was relieved when she held it. "I'm so sorry if it seemed that way, angel. Now that I know it's important, I will never disappear without leaving a note, okay?"

"Then what were those messages about?" she asked. "It really sounded like people were telling you to keep away from me, or just use me as a fling."

The thought that this could be thought of as a casual fling nauseated me. "You're the most amazing woman I've ever met, Lorena. You're beautiful, sweet, and incredibly talented.

I don't give a damn about what anyone says about either of us. Small town gossip comes and goes like waves. All I know is that I love you, and want to be your man."

Her eyes filled with fresh tears, and I realized what I had said without even thinking. But it was the absolute truth. I loved this girl through and through.

Pulling her against my chest, I wrapped her in my arms. "Baby, I can't stand seeing you cry. What can I do?"

"You swear those messages weren't about me being a fat slut?"

I stiffened. "If I hear you say something like that again, I'll be tempted to wash your mouth out with soap," I murmured.

She looked up at me, her eyes absolutely pleading. Skimming my thumb under her eyes, I tried to wipe away her tears. "Angel, if you come outside with me for just a minute, I swear that you'll be happy, and understand everything."

She hesitated, but her head fell against my chest again.

"If I'm wrong, you can punish me however you'd like."

"Okay," she said in a tiny voice. Scooping her up, I pulled her off the counter, holding her tight against me for another moment.

A few eyebrows were raised as we walked out of the ladies room with me holding her hand. I took her straight out the front door, then around to the side parking lot.

"I couldn't stand the thought of you not having your own way to get around, baby," I said. As we turned the corner, she could see a little blue car parked beside my truck. George had driven it here for me, followed by his extremely irritated wife.

"The texts were from George," I explained. "We agreed that you needed a heavier car, to get more traction on these rough back roads, especially when it rains. I test drove three of them, and was going to ask for your opinion, but this one was by far in the best shape, and safest. And I've noticed that a few of your dresses are blue, so I know you like the color."

Lifting her hand, I kissed the back of it. "Your safety is everything to me, angel. This is the project I really had to get done today."

Lorena stared at the car, then at me, back and forth a few times before bursting into tears again. But this time she was grinning, and slightly bouncing up and down. I silently prayed that this was a good sign.

I thought I was going to explode. This whole day had been too much to take. He wanted me to train him to be my boyfriend, and tell him what I wanted from him? He loved me? And he bought me a car?

Falling into his arms in tears, I murmured, "Thank you. Thank you, Cody."

"No, angel, don't cry. Shh."

Rocking in his arms, I took a deep breath as he held me close, forcing myself to calm down. "I'm a complete ass."

"Shh," he murmured, snuggling me into his wide, warm chest. "I should have thought to leave a note. I'm so sorry. That must have put you in a bad state even before you saw those bits of messages. I can't stand that you thought I'd really left."

"You left a note on the door the day before so I wouldn't walk out into the construction," I said softly.

I looked up to see him looking horrified. "Dammit, you're right. But I'm used to construction sites. I've...well, I've never stayed over at a woman's home before. I'm so sorry, baby. I'll never leave without a note again."

"But, a car? What...why?"

"I know you work nights, and I won't always be able to stay so late when I have an early morning job."

"Oh, I'd never expect you to!" I exclaimed. "I get a ride with my coworkers. It's fine."

Cody shook his head. "Yeah, that's fine. Until the day comes when everyone is busy, or you're not quite sure if they had a couple of drinks on their shift. Things happen. That's why I was talking with George yesterday. He said he had some cars that sounded like they'd be great for you, so I rushed down to test them first thing, before he'd even sent me the details."

"Oh, wow. Thanks," I said softly, not quite believing it. "But I really can't put that much on credit."

"Lorena, I bought it for you as a gift," he said, giving me the most adorable, shy smile. "You have to be okay with it, so that I won't worry about you getting home safely every single night." Rocking me gently in his arms again, he murmured, "Honestly, you'll be doing me a big favor. Imagine me tossing and turning, unable to sleep because I'm picturing you stranded."

"Then you're going to have to remember your phone," I said, "so that I can send you messages that I'm home safe."

"I've never forgotten it before," he said sheepishly. "I was standing by the bed, watching you sleep for a moment, thinking about what it would be like to wake up beside you every single morning."

Wow. For a guy who had been so quiet up until the other night, he certainly knew what to say to make a girl's heart light up. I kissed him hard, holding him so tight it surprised me. His arms tightened around me, as we completely forgot where we were for a moment, his tongue against mine, the two of us breathing as one.

Then I jumped. "Oh! I have to get back to work."

"Yes, I'm sorry, baby. Go."

I rushed back inside, doing a quick sweep of all of my tables before Iris came over to where I was opening a fresh bottle of wine. "You say the word, and I'll toss him out myself," she said.

I laughed too loudly, still twitching with relief. "It was all a big misunderstanding."

"You sure?"

Nodding, I whispered, "He bought me a car. So now I can work any shift you like."

"Did he, now?" she smiled widely, looking over to where Cody had just sat down in his usual spot. Iris strolled over, which actually made him look a bit nervous.

"I heard you're taking good care of our girl after all," she said with a grin. "You keep doing that, and keep your arse out of the ladies room, and your first beer's on me."

"Absolutely, ma'am. Dark stout, thank you kindly."

As I rushed fresh glasses of wine to the ladies in the corner, it amused me how formal Iris and Cody were with each other. I guess, in a way, he needed her approval for things to seem proper.

Everything really did seem to be in its place now, except for one tiny detail. Rushing around the room, it took me a while before I could take a break, but Cody seemed patient as ever.

When I finally had a chance to stand close beside him, I whispered, "I'm sorry I was so hysterical. I've never had a boyfriend before, and I had my hopes up way too high for them to be dashed during our first weekend together."

"I understand. We both have a lot to learn, but we'll figure it out."

Bringing my lips to his ear, I breathed, "And I think I love you too."

In a flash, he spun and kissed me. The rest of the world

disappeared. His lips, his hands, Cody breathing me in. At that moment, I knew that he was absolutely the one. It was only a few seconds, but it was life-changing.

He pulled away too soon, but it was understandable since I was at work and we were already getting funny looks. "Actually, I don't think," I whispered. "I know I love you."

"I love you, angel," Cody breathed into my ear. "May I follow you home tonight?"

I nodded, grinning, rushing back to the kitchen. The rest of my shift seemed to take forever, but soon I was driving my very own car home, with Cody's truck right behind me. When we got to my place, there was the perfect amount of space at the end of the driveway for our two vehicles.

As I unlocked the front door, I heard Cody come up behind me, wrapping a hand around my waist. "I'm relieved to see that you're a good driver," he said. "Testing the brakes before you trusted them, going at a very reasonable speed, even though you must know how badly I need to get you naked. You're a very sensible lady, Lorena."

I giggled, then laughed out loud as I realized he wasn't kidding. The door was locked, his boots were off, and I was scooped in his arms, being dropped on the bed in a flash.

Although I don't quite think anything ripped, it felt like he was tearing my clothes off. As soon as we were both naked, his huge body beside mine and his hand on my hip, he kissed me intensely.

"Lorena, I've had to corral a wild horse with my bare hands, deliver a calf with no assistance, and put out a brush-fire with buckets and my boots. But I've never been as scared as I was today when I honestly thought you were going to break up with me."

"I'm sorry I thought the worst," I said. "I guess I've always just expected that people are more likely to believe the bad things about me than the good."

He nodded, his hand reaching behind to cup my ass, squeezing my skin. "I guess I can understand that, but I hate it. You're an amazing girl, and almost everyone in town knows it. The tiny handful of people who don't like you don't like anyone, so they can just go to hell."

We laughed together, then he moved over me, kissing down my neck to nibble at my nipples until I was squirming under him.

During the drive home, I had been hoping for a repeat of last night's amazing experience. But now that his thigh was rubbing over mine, his hand gripping my hip, his lips wrapped around my nipple, I realized that I needed much more than that.

Pulling his shoulder slightly, I brought his lips back to mine. "Sorry, baby," he murmured against my lips. "I didn't mean to assume that you'd want me like that again tonight."

"I do want you, but I also need to tell you…thank you."

"For what, angel?"

I kissed the tip of his nose, making him grin. "For my beautiful new car. It's not just the car itself, which is amazing, but it's what it means to me."

He kissed along my eyebrow. "What does it mean to you?"

"That we're real," I whispered. "This isn't a fling, or a crush, or anything temporary. I want us to be together for good. And knowing how much you want to keep me safe definitely tells me that's what you are thinking as well."

"Lorena, I've never been in a relationship that lasted more than a few weeks, and that was years and years ago. I stopped trying to date because I didn't think anybody was dateable. But then you came along, and you're not just dateable, you're keepable."

I giggled as he kissed along to my ear. "I don't think that's a word," I whispered.

"Okay, I'll use a different word. How about you're lovable. Because I do love you."

It seemed so much more serious with us lying here together, alone and naked. His eyes were on mine, gauging my reaction. I was frozen for only a blink before smiling. "Cody, I love you too."

He exhaled a loud sigh of relief. Then he kissed me. There was something slightly different in his energy, as his arms held me close, and his lips held me captive.

When his lips disappeared, I whimpered in frustration, but then I felt them between my legs. His tongue against my sensitive flesh opened me on levels I wasn't aware I possessed. A humming moan rolled through him as he licked up drops of my arousal. His hunger for me was strange, but devastatingly sexy.

"I love your little pussy," he murmured, flashing me a wink. "I need to feel you come on my tongue again, Lorena."

Hearing Cody, usually so formal and proper, talking dirty, did me in completely. My fingernails dug into his shoulders as he licked my little button steadily. My climax washed over me like rainfall in the desert – hot and desperate and blissful.

Then his huge, muscled body rose up, his lips meeting mine for a kiss so deep it nearly made me dizzy. Feeling his hot, hard length pressing against my mound filled me with a deep, primal ache.

"I need you," I whispered, staring into his eyes until he realized what I meant.

"If you're sure, I'll pick up some condoms tomorrow."

"I'm very sure, and I'm on the pill." I could feel myself blushing again. "It was to straighten out some hormonal issues. I mean, I never needed it before, you know…"

"It's okay, baby," he smiled. "I just want to be damn sure that you are completely certain."

"Eight hundred and thirty-three percent sure," I said.

"That's a weirdly specific number."

"It's the number on the license plate of my new car," I giggled.

I stopped laughing when I realized what this moment meant. My legs spread open, wrapping around his hips. The feeling of the round head of his shaft slipping between my inner lips was almost ticklish, I was so sensitive.

Cody kept his weight on his forearms, leaving his hands free to caress my face, running his fingers through my hair and along my neck while he looked into my eyes. "I love you so much, Lorena," he murmured, sliding inside me slowly.

"I love you, Cody."

As he pressed deeper, he began to work back and forth in slow, smooth movements, opening me carefully without pushing too far at once. The rocking movement of his hips was so arousing that I felt myself becoming even wetter.

It was downright weird feeling like my body was stretching open for him, and I forced myself to hold back a yelp when he passed a certain point.

I couldn't let him know that it hurt, and indeed as soon as he was all the way inside me, taking slow, steady strokes, the few rough spots turned into pure bliss. He moved in an unwavering rhythm, rolling his hips as he rocked us together.

His eyes half-closed for a moment. "Lorena," he moaned, "My sweet angel. You really are perfect for me in every single way."

I could already feel my core beginning to quiver, the pressure building. As he stared into my eyes, I felt like my entire body and soul were melting.

He quickened the pace gradually, his thrusts growing deeper, more savage. Somehow he expertly brought me right to the edge so that he knew the second I tumbled over, shrieking his name.

"Yes, angel…yes!" he growled, following me a split second later as we came in each other's arms.

After the last tremors rolled through us, his instant grin was pure joy to me. Rolling onto his back beside me, he held my hand sweetly as we caught our breath together.

"I had no idea," I finally murmured.

"Neither did I," he said. "For the record, it is not normal for two people to click so perfectly right away as we do."

"Everything has been a bit fast," I smiled.

He squeezed my hand, looking at me with concern. "Not too fast, I hope?"

I shook my head. "Sometimes things are sudden, but it doesn't mean it's not right. On Thursday I would never have thought that I was ready to sing in front of a crowd. Then Friday was a bit of a surprise, and Saturday was a little emergency. I guess these things just happen."

"You are my little emergency," he chuckled, his low voice so sexy when it rumbled. "I was just at the point where I was wondering what the hell I was going to do with the rest of my life. Whether I should get new animals for my farm, start raising cattle again, or buy some new tools and expand my construction business."

"So…what are you going to do now?" I asked, turning to lean up on my elbow.

"Whatever is right for both of us," he said. "You could move in with me, and we could farm there. But since this is your grandmother's old place, you probably want to stay here."

"I'd like to, if possible," I said.

"Anything is possible, baby," he smiled, running his fingers along my spine. "I could buy a couple of the fields next door, and we could start an organic farm. Just easy things like chickens and spinach and peppers. I'll have to fix up part of this house first, of course."

"Now that I have a car, I can work more shifts, and longer shifts, to pay for the supplies," I said.

Cody shook his head. "No, you're going to be too busy looking for a band to sing with. I'm not going to have you ignore your dreams. That absolutely comes first. The rest of it, we'll just figure out as we go."

I couldn't help giggling. "I'm glad that I've started to figure you out," I said. "You were so quiet at first that I didn't know whether I could get to know you."

"You brought me out of my shell," he said. "Like singing brings you out of yours."

"Maybe we shouldn't raise chickens if we're breaking eggshells left and right," I smiled.

His fingers began making light circles and patterns across the back of my shoulder blades. "I'm going to try really hard to leave a note in the morning, but I have to do an early job. So I'll be gone for a few hours, then come back here, okay?"

"Just don't forget your phone this time. That way I can text you and clear up misunderstandings before they start."

"Well, you're going to have to stop being so damn beautiful while you're sleeping. If I get all flustered and distracted, that could hardly be my fault. I'm just a man, after all."

"There you go, wanting to change me already," I laughed.

Cody nuzzled my throat, then gently pulled my bottom lip between his teeth playfully. "The only thing I'm ever going to change about you, angel, is our living arrangements, and the lack of a ring on your pretty little finger."

I felt my eyes nearly popping out of my head. "It's a bit early for that, don't you think?"

"That's why I'm warning you slightly in advance, because it's going to be quick," he smiled.

He turned off the bedside lamp, pulling a blanket over us as he snuggled me into his shoulder. "I can't imagine ever trying to sleep without you in my arms again," he said softly,

"And I don't want any gossip about us living in sin. So prepare to be engaged before the end of the month, angel."

I wasn't quite sure if he was teasing or exaggerating, but it didn't matter. I'm sure that he could tell by the way my body fit against his, my hand over his heart, that I was going to say yes.

~ TWO YEARS LATER ~

I thought the air always felt electrified during a show. Everyone in the huge downtown club was there to have a mellow night, but singing with the band was always incredibly exciting to me.

Each band had been special in its own way, as I had sung with a few different groups over the past two years. But once Bobby's wife was expecting their second child, I officially became a "Well-Behaved Outlaw" last year. Except I wasn't just singing backup anymore, I was now the lead singer on about two-thirds of the set.

We also weren't just doing cover songs – we were now getting together and writing our own songs as well. It was an absolute blast to write old fashioned country heart-wrenchers about modern things, like the song I wrote, "The text that nearly tore us apart."

Luckily, Cody thought the song was hilarious. As I sang it for him, and several hundred other people tonight, he had raised his coffee mug, giving me a big thumbs up.

As I started to introduce our last song of the night, I glanced around to smile at the band. They had all been very understanding when Cody had come to my first rehearsal to meet them. I'd been a bit nervous about it, but he had simply shaken everyone's hand in that strangely formal way of his, reassured that I was working on a project with quality men.

They were all ranch hands and farmers as well, except for Bobby, who was a mechanic for specialized farm equipment like tractors and combines.

Playing Wednesday and Thursday nights in the city messed up their early morning schedules, but everyone survived. The money wasn't great, but it brought so much happiness to so many people. It was also the most fun in the world.

As I lifted the microphone, the stage lights bounced off my wedding ring, making the diamonds sparkle even more.

"For the last song, I think we're going to do an old number by everyone's Uncle Kenny," I said, making everyone howl with laughter. It was charming that everyone knew the oldies, and even decades after they were written, still sang along. They were always there, in the back of our minds somehow. Steadying us.

As I began to sing, I even saw Cody singing along a bit from his seat on a stool at the end of the bar. He didn't come to all of our shows but made it out at least once or twice a month.

The audience went wild tonight. They seemed to love it when I sang songs that were intended for a man to sing to a woman. I didn't bother flipping the genders, I just sang it the way it had been written. By the time I was finished, the entire room was positively grinning.

"Well, it sounds like those people were caught in a hard place at a bad time, but it sure makes for a great song, right folks?" Everyone applauded and laughed. Then I turned to the deep, shining eyes that were fixated on me. It was a little early to be sharing my big news, but I couldn't hold it in any longer. Although I was nervous, I was pretty sure that now was the time.

"Cody, don't you think that Lucille would be a lovely name if it's a girl?"

The entire crowd laughed, but then grew quiet as my hand fluttered to my stomach. Cody seemed to freeze, then stood up slowly, walking toward me with the biggest grin I'd ever seen outside of our wedding day.

Bobby leaned into his mic. "And if it's a boy, it had better be named Johnny, Hank, Willie, or Waylon. Congratulations Lorena and Cody!"

Snapping my mic back into the stand, I left Bobby to say good night to the crowd, rushing to sit at the front edge of the stage so I could jump into Cody's arms.

He twirled me around a few times, and the cheers were deafening. Then my husband just held me close, murmuring into my ear, "You're really giving me a baby?"

"You've already given me so much, I thought it was only fair," I laughed. My eyes were misty as I looked up at him. "I love you so much, Cody."

"I love you eight hundred and thirty-three times as much, Lorena," he smiled. His jaw was actually twitching on the left side, and although I would never admit to having seen a glimmer of a tear, his eyes certainly looked glassy for a second. "I love you, my sweet wife, and soon to be mommy."

Cody and I had driven together tonight, so I gave Bobby a wave, knowing that he would understand if just this once I was a diva who didn't help with packing the gear. As we went to Cody's truck, he practically threw me inside so that he could jump in and shut the door.

His kiss was pure fire, and I couldn't help wondering what would happen the second we got home to our quirky little house.

Cody had moved in with me after only dating for a

month. I was pretty pleased with myself for making a big deal out of handing him a key to my house, but he outdid me by slipping a diamond ring on my finger.

He renovated parts of the house completely, but others he simply fixed up a bit, and left them with their old country charm. While he was doing the heavy reno lifting, I designed the wildflower and vegetable gardens in the huge backyard, which is where we had our wedding.

It was small and charming and quiet. Exactly what we both wanted. The only bad thing that happened on our perfect day was that during the reception at The Last Barrel, I kept getting in trouble for jumping up and clearing the plates.

Cody's kiss brought me back to reality, his hand grabbing my ass almost roughly as he squeezed my breasts with his other hand right through my dress. "When these get bigger, your little stage dresses are going to be obscene," he said, his low voice sounding strained.

"Gosh," I joked, "A blonde country singer with giant breasts. Who knows how that might turn out?"

His lips crushed to mine before he could even laugh properly, his tongue sliding over my own as we became lost in each other. He pulled away far too soon. "Seatbelt," he muttered, buckling his own. I sat close beside him as he drove out of the lot, knowing that we would be home in record time.

Looking over at him, I saw that the lust in his eyes had been replaced with something else. "What's wrong?" I asked as he turned onto the highway.

"How do you feel about me putting my extension on the house?" he asked. "The basement isn't really tall enough for a proper playroom."

"Babies and toddlers are pretty short," I said. "Low ceilings are going to be fine for them for at least ten years."

He chuckled, and thankfully relaxed his foot on the gas a little.

"I love you so much, Lorena," he said, holding my hand. As we drove past ranch after ranch toward our beautiful small town, and our gorgeous little house, I realized that I was still pretty nervous about having a child.

But I'd been nervous to speak to Cody at first. And I'd been nervous to sing on stage the first several dozen times. Whatever happened, I knew with absolute certainty that I could get through anything with him at my side.

"Don't you fall asleep on me," Cody chuckled.

"Not a chance," I said softly. "I wouldn't want to miss a single thing."

the end

Keep reading for a preview of
Her New Bodyguard.

HER NEW BODYGUARD: JACKSON

I looked in the rear view mirror. It was getting harder to see the cars behind me as it grew darker, but it felt like that gray sedan had been behind me for a very long time.

Slowing down even more, I figured that he would eventually pass me. Yet he didn't come any closer, matching his speed to mine perfectly as he stayed behind me, with a little blue pickup between us.

Should I be concerned? Was I being tailed? I was about to call my brother Kevin to have him meet me when my phone rang.

"Hello?"

"Ashley, this is Jackson. I'm from the Barrow Agency - your father's new security team. I need you to listen, please. We have reason to believe that someone might be following you. Are you on the highway right now?"

"Yes..." Something about his no-nonsense tone made me believe him, but he also could have been some crackpot. "Wait. How can I know that you got my number from Dad?" I asked.

"Your first pet was a white kitten named Ducky. Your

favorite childhood meal was something you called 'red soup with stuff in it'. Your bedsheets are always purple. Mr. Avalon told me all this so that you would know that he sent me. Okay?"

I wasn't sure whether I should be embarrassed that a strange man seemed to know my personal business. There was no way any of that information was online anywhere. "Okay."

"Have you noticed a gray midsize car following you at any point?"

My spine turned to ice. "He's practically right behind me. Has been for a while."

There was a muffled curse. "Where are you, precisely?"

"I'm headed into Oakton now. I just passed Stanley's service station about a minute ago."

"I'm close to your location. Hold on." I heard some quick tapping on a computer.

"The next exit is 108. Keep slowing down, and admire the scenery. Take the exit at the last possible second that you can do so safely. When you're off the highway, turn north and floor it for half a mile until you see Edmond Road."

"Okay." I could already see the exit up ahead, and felt my pulse racing as I slowly took my foot off the gas.

"You're going to turn right on Edmund, then right again into the second driveway you see. You'll be mostly hidden by farm buildings. Look for the open garage door. Drive right in and turn the van off."

"Got it."

Even though I was driving slowly, the exit was fast approaching. The blue truck was practically on my tail, and I couldn't quite see the gray car behind him.

"It's going to be fine, Ashley," the gruff, deep voice said soothingly. "As soon as you're in the garage, I'll be able to protect you."

"Okay."

I moved quickly into the exit lane, and the gray car missed the turn. Then he slammed on the brakes to back up around the concrete barrier. But I was already gone, taking the ramp as fast as I dared.

"You're doing great, Ashley," he said. "Smooth driving. The gray car was blocked by a transport truck, so he's going to be stuck for a minute."

"How can you see me?" I asked.

Again, that deep chuckle. "I'm not permitted to tell you that I have a drone camera, which is a shame. I have a feeling that might make you feel better right now."

"You're right, it does." I was so nervous that it was hard to take a full breath.

I barely paused at the stop sign, then pressed the gas pedal nearly to the floor. Kevin's old van groaned, then went faster than I would have ever expected it to.

"Doing great, Ashley. Only a few more minutes."

North, then right, then right again into the driveway and I was suddenly parked in a barn with the door closing behind me even as I ended the call. I jumped out of the van and looked around, wondering whether I should grab a crowbar or something to try to protect myself.

A tall shadow came toward me. "Well done, Ashley."

It was the same deep voice from the phone call. He stepped into the dim glow of the single lightbulb over us. "Pleased to meet you. I'm Jackson."

Holy crap. The man was gorgeous. And huge. *Wow.* I would have been afraid of him if I met him in a dark alley and he hadn't just saved me from some unknown stalker. There was a faint scar along his temple that made him even sexier.

As he held out his hand to shake mine, I was still fluttering like a leaf. He took both of my hands, then led me over to two battered lawn chairs near a workbench in the far corner.

"It's okay," he said, drawing the chairs closer together and sitting us down. "It's over. Just breathe."

Her New Bodyguard is available in paperback now - look for the Paperbacks page at www.haleytravisromance.com

the good luck kiss from a stranger, but isn't falling in love so fast just a fantasy?

Fake Summer Boyfriend

I'm terrified of giant men. But when Leif volunteered to scare off my stalker by pretending to be my boyfriend, I knew the gorgeous hulking security tech was the perfect man for the job.

The Last Date

I was infatuated with Sasha. I will tease her, even court her, until I make her mine. Forever.

Please join the mailing list at

www.haleytravisromance.com

for new releases, updates, discounts & freebies!